Also by Susan Gabriel

Fiction

The Secret Sense of Wildflower
(a Kirkus Reviews' Best Book of 2012)

Lily's Song
(sequel to *The Secret Sense of Wildflower*)

Trueluck Summer

Temple Secrets

Seeking Sara Summers

Circle of the Ancestors

Quentin & the Cave Boy

Nonfiction

Fearless Writing for Women:
Extreme Encouragement & Writing Inspiration

Available at all booksellers
in print, ebook and audio formats.

Grace, Grits and Ghosts

Southern Short Stories

Susan Gabriel

Wild Lily Arts

Grace, Grits and Ghosts

Copyright © 2015 by Susan Gabriel

ISBN 978-0-9835882-8-3

Table of Contents

Introduction

When I became a writer twenty years ago, I swore that I would never, ever write southern fiction. Perhaps it was because I had more than a few odd southern characters in my gene pool that I would have liked to forget. Like many with young and rebellious spirits, I wanted to divorce myself from the South and from its sometimes backward ways and write literary fiction set in other locations. Distant places I'd only visited, instead of the ones I'd been rooted in. And, like many of us, what I set out to avoid is exactly what I found myself doing.

My "never say never" moment happened in the middle of the night one summer many years ago (about six years after I'd made that promise) when a character by the name of Louisa May "Wildflower" McAllister started talking to me out of a dream. I heard her voice as clearly as my own. Since I am a writer, and also a Southerner, I figure I get to be a little crazy, so I hesitated only momentarily before I started writing down what she told me and continued to do so in the weeks and months that followed.

Over a decade later those writings became my novel, *The Secret Sense of Wildflower*. To my delight, the book was given a starred review by the esteemed Kirkus Reviews, which named it to their Best Book of 2012 list. I also have a short story by the same name, the last story in this collection. *The Secret Sense of Wildflower* is considered southern gothic, or southern historical fiction, although any true Southerner would call it normal, everyday life.

One of the things that makes southern fiction "southern" is its sense of place. Not only are the characters quirky and sometimes bigger than life, but they are also grounded in the landscape. Throw in a crackpot, an old wise woman and a preacher, and we love it even more. We southerners, those born-and-raised like me, as well as transplants from all over the world, love our countryside.

Abandoned houses, cemeteries, eccentric relatives, even murderers and rapists show up in southern gothic fiction. These tales contain flawed, bigger-than-life characters—characters who are quirky, intense, and often commit a necessary sin to set them firmly on the path to seeking redemption. Or not.

Southern gothic fiction is packed with mystery, rooted in the landscape where the South itself is a character that is haunted by the past. Ghosts show up to remind us of our history, and perhaps our need to transform it.

The eight short stories in *Grace, Grits and Ghosts: Southern Short Stories* are set in the southeastern United States and have their share of quirky, poignant and deep characters.

Temple Secrets takes place in a mansion in Savannah, Georgia and is narrated by Queenie, the funny half-sister of Iris Temple, a prominent Savannah matriarch. Please note that it is also the only story in my twenty-year writing career that contains several occurrences of flatulence. Forgive me. I kept trying to edit it out, but—like Iris—it refused to go away. This short story is also adapted from a longer work, a novel by the same name. Novelists, like me, frequently create a short story from a longer work, just as short story writers often turn one of their short pieces into a novel.

The Mail Slot is set in another old mansion, this one past its glory days, in Atlanta, Georgia. The main character, Allison Whitworth, fears leaving her house. As a former psychotherapist, my stories often have characters with interesting psychological traits. This story came to me during a writer's workshop with Marge Piercy.

The End was first published in *Cease, Cows* literary journal, and is a piece of flash fiction, a short, short story. After I experienced a hot flash in the middle of the night, I awoke to write this flash fiction (no pun intended) told by a man who just turned fifty. I get some of my best characters from dreams.

Gullah Secrets takes place in the 1960s on an island off the coast of South Carolina and is told in the voice of Old Sally, a Gullah woman whose mother was a slave. This is also a story pulled from the novel, *Temple Secrets,* so you will read about some of the same characters you met in the first short story in this collection.

Country Obituary - #1 is another work of flash fiction and takes place in the fictional small town of Jacob's Ridge in North Carolina. I wrote it specifically for this short story collection after being inspired by an obituary in our small town newspaper.

Country Obituary – #2 After reading *Country Obituary – #1*, you may find this obituary especially poignant. I created these characters from my imagination, however they feel like they might have lived right down the road. I wish I'd known them in real life.

River Reunion is the newest short story in the collection and is more representative of what I like to think of as the *new* South. The characters—four women in their seventies—have already been through the rough stuff and are well on their way to transformation. I hope you love these gals as much as I do.

Scarlett & Rhett Redux is another flash fiction story, told by a male narrator who comes upon an elderly couple pushing a baby carriage. Something similar happened to me, although I came across them on a walking trail in the North Carolina mountains. I changed the setting to historic St. Augustine,

Florida, simply because that's where my imagination wanted to go with it. This story is an example of southern humor.

The Secret Sense of Wildflower (a short story based on the book by the same name) is historical fiction, set in the Appalachian mountains of 1940s Tennessee. It is narrated by a resilient and courageous 12-year-old girl nicknamed Wildflower as she comes of age and faces danger, death and new life.

With the exception of the three years I lived in Colorado, I have lived in the Southeastern United States my entire life. I grew up in Knoxville, Tennessee, in the foothills of the Great Smoky Mountains. Then as an adult I lived in Charleston, South Carolina for fourteen years. After Hurricane Hugo's devastation, I went searching for higher ground and ended up in Asheville, North Carolina.

Since 2009 I have lived in the small town of Brevard, NC, nestled in the arms of the Blue Ridge Mountains, a place known for waterfalls, forests and hiking trails. A place that houses not only a fine liberal arts college, but an internationally renowned music festival. A place with mountain bikers, white squirrels, and a squirrelly character or two. I study them all to get new material for my stories.

Some may look disdainfully at the South's sleepy little towns. But in a nation that is sleep-deprived, stressed-out, and searching for answers, a little slower pace makes sense. It's

true, we have a different rhythm here. It is the rhythm of waterfalls, mountain streams and walks by the river, of a front
porch welcoming locals and visitors alike to ponder their place
and purpose on earth.

It wasn't until I left the South that I realized how deeply
southern I am. I love shade. I love moss growing on trees, and
the warm, humid breezes that flow along the southern coasts.
I love people who take the time to ponder, mosey, and sit a
spell. I am one of those people.

As I sit here overlooking the Blue Ridge Mountains, located in one of the most lush and bio-diverse areas in the
world, I invite you to read these stories and let the land speak
to you. Even if you're not from around here, you will catch a
glimpse of a special place. A place where Native Americans
thought the story of creation began. A place that gave birth to
the third oldest river in the world. A place that I love and call
home.

I hope you enjoy *Grace, Grits and Ghosts: Southern Short Stories.* Please consider letting me know what you think by writing
a review on Amazon and Goodreads. Or you can email me.
I'm easy to find. Either way I'd love to hear from you.

--- Susan Gabriel

Temple Secrets

(a short story based on the novel)

Iris Temple had been threatening to die for three decades and most of the people in Savannah who knew her, wanted her to get on with it. Queenie looked up from the crime novel she'd hidden within the pages of *Southern Living* magazine and took in the figure across the sun room of her half-sister, Iris Temple. Everything about Iris spoke of privilege: the posture, the clothes, the understated jewels. Not to mention a level of entitlement that made Queenie's head ache. An exasperated moan slipped from her mouth before she could catch it.

Iris's gaze shifted to Queenie and her eyes narrowed, the adjoining crow's feet forming a close-knit flock. The look delivered the message that even though Queenie was solidly middle-aged, she was to be *seen and not heard* like a child.

As Iris Temple's companion for the last thirty-five years, Queenie lived the lifestyle of a Temple, instead of a Temple servant like her mother, grandmother and great grandmother. With the precision of a Swiss clock, Queenie was reminded daily that she was not a *true* Temple—though they shared the same father—any more than Sunny Delight orange drink was considered *real* orange juice. She was simply a watered-down Temple—albeit several shades darker.

Every morning, Iris studied the local newspaper in the lavish sun room facing the prominent Savannah square. Wicker furniture with rich fabrics mingled among antiques and tropical plants, as gold elephants the size of laundry baskets offered their polished backs to hold Iris's porcelain teacup.

Focused on the society section, Iris licked her lips as though relishing the fact that the Temples were one of the elite Savannah families. Her photograph appeared in the newspaper with a regularity that her bowels rarely achieved. As if on cue, Iris's stomach gurgled and she shifted her weight onto one hip and rose ever so slightly to produce the noxious result. Queenie might have felt sorry for Iris if she were treated more kindly. Instead, she bit her tongue to keep from saying:

Iris, honey, they say humans pass gas 14 times a day, but you hold the Guinness Book of World Records!

For years, Iris Temple's unpredictable illnesses, usually of a gastrointestinal nature, manipulated everyone around her. Just last week, a stomachache had canceled a Daughter's of the Confederacy charity event and gas pains dismantled a family reunion planned for over a decade. Any societal unpleasantness was quickly dissipated with a severe attack of acid reflux, followed by an acute bout of flatulence, guaranteed to clear any gathering. To what did Iris Temple attribute these ailments? Gullah voodoo.

Within seconds, the odor's flight path reached Queenie and she held her breath as Iris turned the page.

"Oh my word, listen to this," Iris said, oblivious to her own fumes. She waited for Queenie to raise her eyes and then began to read.

"Miss Iris Temple, of the Savannah Temples, will be hosting the 20th annual charity bazaar for the Junior League on this coming Saturday. The grand matriarch, also known as Savannah's grandmother--" Iris balked and looked as though she'd swallowed something bitter. "Savannah's grandmother? Is that supposed to be a compliment?"

"Oh, I'm sure it is, Iris," Queenie answered, all the while thinking, *never mind that you have only one grandchild you've never even met and don't have a nurturing bone in your body.*

Queenie anticipated what would follow: Iris's angry letter to the newspaper on gold embossed Temple stationary that would insist the reporter be dismissed, and Queenie ordered to deliver the bad news.

Voodoo or not, most people—including Queenie—considered Iris Temple a first class fake. What she blamed on folk magic was merely an excuse to bring the fancy families and institutions of Savannah under her control.

And if that doesn't work, there's always that damn ledger, kept in a safe deposit box at the bank, Queenie thought. A ledger that documented hundreds of secrets about different Savannah families. Secrets their great-grandfather Cyrus Temple had begun collecting before the Civil War, and that every Temple had contributed to since.

Well, not every Temple, Queenie thought. *Iris has never asked my thoughts on anything, never mind what I'd like to put in that secret book.*

Iris had noted every affair of prominent men, their illegitimate children, mental illnesses of wives, and any dishonest money dealings she'd ever been privy to. According to Iris, Queenie had two entire pages devoted to her. Given the Temple family's inclination to lie if it benefited them, Queenie questioned how many of those so called secrets were true.

Lunch was served in the dining room, a room that could easily pass as a stage set for a BBC mini-series. Iris sat at the head of the elongated table while Queenie took her place at the far end of the mahogany monster, a safe distance away from any future gastrointestinal distress.

"Did you call the restaurant about tonight?" Iris asked.

"Yes, Iris, it's all been arranged," she said, already bored with the litany of questions sure to follow. Meanwhile, Queenie nibbled on what passed for grass but was really watercress and glanced at her half-sister seated at the other end of the table.

Only you, Iris, would counteract a voodoo curse by following a strict diet consisting of no sauces, no spices, and no intermingling of foods. You might as well eat the Temple Book of Secrets!

Part of Queenie's job as Iris's assistant was to make certain that chefs in downtown establishments followed her strict dietary restrictions. Queenie knew chefs didn't like to be told what to do. But if any failed to meet Iris's requirements, Iris made sure they never worked in Savannah again.

"And did you tell them about my special condition?" Iris's pinkie finger saluted the chandelier as she ate a bland-looking soup. "You know how delicate I am," she added. "Fragrances make me nauseous."

"Yes, Iris. I made them aware," Queenie said, thinking Iris was about as *delicate* as a piranha.

Fragrances included perfumes and scented body powders, soaps, shampoos and detergents. Every maître d' in town had been alerted not to sit Iris next to anyone who might fall under the scrutiny of her superior olfactory system.

After swallowing another mouthful, Iris asked, "What about the Catholic charities meeting tomorrow?" She forked in some salad sans dressing.

"I'll see to it, Iris." Queenie had to resist rolling her eyes. *It would be more of a charity for Savannah if Iris didn't show up,* she thought.

For the privilege of living in the big house as Iris Temple's companion, Queenie cringed at the price demanded of her. Among other things, she was required to arrive thirty minutes early to every meeting of the Junior League, the Daughters of the Confederacy and any other event that Iris Temple was scheduled to attend to ensure that they were fragrance free.

On those days, Queenie felt like little more than a trained bloodhound, sniffing at the heels of Savannah's elite. More than once Queenie had approached prominent Savannah residents to request they go to the restroom and scrub off expensive perfumes. This seldom went over well, leaving Queenie to feel darker than she already was.

Queenie knew how the rich women of Savannah felt about her. She had overheard their whispers, their cutting remarks about her color, her place. No matter what she did, they—like Iris—would never see her as legitimate. They would never see her for the woman she was. And of course they never considered the burden Queenie carried because of Iris's insistence that she play Prissy to her Scarlett O'Hara, simply to have a decent existence.

Yet deep down Queenie knew she was as entitled to her life as Iris was, as well as what their daddy left behind when he passed over.

"I smelled one of those horrible dryer sheets yesterday," she began again, her nose upturned. The clicking of Iris's spoon against the soup bowl competed with the grating sound of her voice.

Queenie sighed. Besides listening to the incessant demands of her half-sister, the worst part of her job involved the periodic sleuth for scents as she strolled the affluent Savannah square where the Temple house stood. During this surveillance, she made certain the housekeepers in the area weren't using scented dryer sheets. Otherwise, said housekeepers risked losing their jobs and their employers risked having their secrets revealed. Secrets Iris had told them were stored in the bank vault.

As a result, most of Savannah—regardless of race, class, gender or age—was waiting on Iris Temple to die. If for no other reason, so that life could return to scented bliss. This thought had certainly passed through Queenie's mind many times. If she were lucky—sooner rather than later—Iris could become one of the many ghosts that lived in the old mansion. She imagined Iris would be a lot easier to live with in spirit form, although the Temple ghosts could get rambunctious from time to time.

"I know it doesn't bother you to smell the dryer sheets," Iris conceded. "But if you were a *true* Temple, you'd understand. You just don't have our level of sophistication."

There it is, Queenie thought, *as predictable as Old Faithful, and just as full of toxic vapors.*

To distract herself from doing Iris harm, Queenie thought back to when she came to live here in 1965, thirty-five years ago. She had been twenty-two years old at the time and Iris, forty-five. It had been Mister Oscar's idea—Iris Temple's husband—that Queenie join the staff because of a special fondness he had for her. A fondness that eventually extended to the bedroom. Back then, Queenie's mother still worked for the Temples as head housekeeper, though she eventually retired and was replaced in 1980 by Violet, Queenie's niece.

At one hundred years of age, Queenie's mother, Old Sally, still practiced the family trade of root doctoring and folk magic in the way her Gullah ancestors did. People came from all over the southeast to have her work her spells and cure illnesses. The Gullah ways were taught to her by Queenie's great-grandmother, Sadie, a slave owned by the Temple family. Queenie had never practiced the family trade. Perhaps it was the Temple blood in her that refused to participate. Though lately, she had questioned if her mother's folk magic might offer a more permanent solution to her arrogant half-sister.

Voodoo aside, every Wednesday afternoon, Queenie accompanied Iris Temple to the Piggly Wiggly grocery store on the opposite end of Savannah. Though she could afford a multitude of chauffeurs, Iris insisted on driving herself—an excursion which always proved harrowing, despite the snail-paced speed. As far as Queenie could tell, Iris had never once used the rear-view or side mirrors on her black Lincoln Town Car. Not to mention, she used the sidewalks in town as a kind of bumper car railing, to keep track of the edge of the road, due to a horrible case of near-sightedness she was too vain to correct. What Iris lacked in accuracy she made up for in spite and anyone she endangered with her recklessness, she deemed somehow deserving.

All household errands were relegated to Queenie, with the exception of this one, which Iris did herself. This errand was to order exotic meats from Spud Grainger, the butcher at the Piggly Wiggly, with whom Iris had had a storied affair in the 1970s. An affair—Iris told Queenie in 1983, after having too much sherry on All Souls Day—that she blamed on an article she'd read in *Vogue Magazine* concerning the free love movement.

The affair had begun in the late 70s, two years after her husband, Oscar, died unexpectedly of a massive heart attack. At the time, Spud Grainger was a bag boy at the Piggly Wiggly and a part-time jazz musician. The affair ended after six months, at Iris Temple's insistence. Heartbroken, Spud Grainger was said to have never played the saxophone again.

Now, twenty or so years later, Iris entered the Piggly Wiggly with the sophistication of Savannah royalty. Queenie followed not far behind. They walked down aisle number three toward the meat department in the back of the store. Despite being eighty years of age, Iris's posture was impeccable, as if a flag pole extended from crown to coccyx. And though she was of normal height—perhaps five feet, seven inches—she seemed much taller than everyone else. Even her wrinkles appeared in proper alignment, and her solid white hair coiffed to perfection, as if she and the Queen of England shared hairdressers.

Queenie served no particular function on these outings except to fulfill her half-sister duty as companion and to keep her mouth shut. Afterward, she would get her hair washed and relaxed at the *Gladys Knight and the Tints* Beauty Parlor located in the shopping center adjacent to the Piggly Wiggly—a reward she looked forward to every week.

Iris arrived at the meat counter gingerly clearing her throat to get Spud Grainger's attention. When this didn't work, Iris's query made a crescendo until the aging butcher turned and smiled. If ever there were an example of love's blindness, it was Spud Grainger's affection for Iris Temple.

"My dear Iris, you get more beautiful every day," he said, his southern accent smooth and lilting.

"How very kind of you, Mister Grainger." Iris radiated a smile that had received very little exercise over the years and her bottom lip quivered with the effort. Once weekly, Queenie marveled at her half-sister's transformation into a somewhat pleasant human being while in Spud Grainger's presence.

Spud Grainger was not a day over sixty and had aged well. A solid white mustache hid his slightly crooked front teeth. He also had an affinity for bow ties. Today's tie was lime green, with thin red stripes that matched the beef tips on special, displayed in the glass case in front of him.

The elegant butcher wiped his hands on his perfectly clean white apron and stepped into the aisle to kiss Iris's extended hand. A girlish giggle escaped her octogenarian lips.

When Queenie was unsuccessful in hiding her smile, Iris shot her a look that could stop a wildebeest in a dead run. Queenie suppressed a gulp as Iris returned her attention to Spud. Iris's face colored slightly from Spud's attention. She tilted her head upward as if this regal gesture might command the color to recede. They spoke affectionately of the weather.

Damn, y'all, how many different ways can you describe hot? Queenie wondered, for Savannah was as hot as a furnace in Hades for six months out of the year and had enough humidity to generate buckets of sweat within seconds.

Iris turned and handed Queenie her leopard handbag, heavy enough to contain the wildebeest. As instructed, Queenie reached inside the bag for a linen envelope containing the neatly written order on Temple stationary. She handed the paper to Spud Grainger, who thanked her kindly.

Exotic meats, Iris told anyone who had the misfortune to ask, were the only thing her delicate, *voodoo cursed*, constitution could tolerate. Whether the strong medicine of these animals was meant to counteract the voodoo spell she was at the mercy of remained a mystery.

Antelope, alligator, buffalo, elk, kangaroo and ostrich were flown in from all over the world at great expense. Not to mention, iguana, llama, rattlesnake and yak. *Animals that would have fought harder,* Queenie thought, *if they knew their capture would result in ending up in Iris Temple's gullet.*

Spud Grainger studied the list. He smiled and petted his mustache, as if Iris Temple's exotic orders, as well as her exotic nature, had captivated him.

"The caribou may take a while," he said thoughtfully. "But I'll give Violet a call as soon as it comes in."

A line of Savannah housewives formed behind Iris Temple. She eyed their khaki shorts and New Balance sneakers and inclined her chin heavenward as if on the trail of an unacceptable scent. She wrinkled her nose, furrowed her brow. Though the 4th of July was three months away, Queenie anticipated the upcoming fireworks.

"Someone is wearing Chanel!" Iris said to Queenie in a whisper that could be heard from the front of the store. The look on Iris's face was one of complete and utter disgust.

Chanel no. 5, as Queenie had been told countless times, was the fragrance of the terminally middle class. Iris Temple abhorred the wannabe rich, or any other kind of rich that didn't involve money that had been around since the disbanding of the Confederacy.

Spud Grainger offered Iris an apologetic look. He motioned to the line forming behind her. Iris stopped mid-sniff and thanked him, another kindness reserved only for Spud. Then she turned to the gaggle of Savannah housewives and huffed her disapproval, giving them a parting hiss, like the rattlesnake she planned to eat for dinner that night. Though Queenie offered a parting apology to the women, the final word came from Iris in a cloud of flatulence that cleared the entire cereal aisle as she departed and sent two giggling children running in search of their mother.

After the Piggly Wiggly, Iris dropped Queenie off at the hairdressers, and then the grand matriarch drove off to conduct another errand. She was never to question the nature of

Iris Temple's other business, but just last week when returning to the car to retrieve her knitting, Queenie had found a bucket of Kentucky Fried Chicken bones crammed under the back seat. The bones had been picked clean, as if an exotic jungle animal had been feasting on them while lying on the plush leather seats.

So much for voodoo and special diets, Queenie had thought at the time, as she held the bucket of bones and smiled back at Colonel Sanders' emblazoned image. If Iris kept this up, hardening of the arteries might take her out, but Queenie wasn't sure she had the fortitude to wait for natural causes.

An hour later, with her hair relaxed and styled, Queenie put the charge on Iris's bill and waited at the entrance of the beauty shop. Within minutes, the shiny black Lincoln rounded the corner, rolled over a part of the sidewalk, and hit a green trash can that bounced off a silver Toyota wagon before coming to rest at the north end of the parking lot.

Good lord, Queenie thought, *this woman is an accident waiting to happen.*

Someday Queenie would have to take the car keys away from Iris, an action she looked forward to about as much as back-to-back root canals. Iris was not the type to give up control of anything, especially large, life-threatening motor vehicles.

Queenie was an exceptional driver herself. Oscar, Iris's husband, had taught her when she was sixteen in an equally big Lincoln Continental. In exchange for the driving lessons, she had agreed to climb into the back seat with him and show him her breasts. At the time, this gesture had seemed a small price to pay for use of the Temple cars. Of course, this was a secret Queenie doubted would ever make it into Iris's precious book.

The Town Car rounded the final corner and veered in Queenie's direction, as if Iris was intent on playing a game of geriatric "chicken." Queenie debated whether to jump aside, but decided to hold her ground.

"Just try it, old lady," Queenie said, her teeth gritted in determination. She locked her ample knees in place, grateful she had some substance to her. "If it's my fate to go to the Great Beyond at the hands of Iris Temple, then so be it," she added. "But I refuse to be the first one to flinch."

The Lincoln screeched to a halt, stopping only inches away from Queenie, so close that heat drifted from the engine and further relaxed her hair. She unlocked her knees and got inside while Iris's wrinkled lips glistened in the sunlight from her latest rendezvous with the Colonel. The smell of his secret recipe of eleven herbs and spices permeated the closed car.

After several attempts, Iris coerced the car into drive and hit the curb twice before reaching the main road, causing a family of four to frantically scatter into the good hands of an Allstate Insurance office.

"God in heaven," Queenie shrieked. "Watch where you're going, Iris!"

"Keep your commandments to yourself," Iris said with a polished sneer. Then she raised one hip to expel another one for the record books.

After returning from dinner later that evening, Iris was not herself. She didn't complain once about their meal. Nor did she create a mundane task for Queenie to do to prove who was in charge. Uncharacteristically, Iris announced in the foyer that she was retiring early and gave Queenie a quick, tight embrace in a rare act of affection that felt more like a frontal Heimlich maneuver. Queenie emitted a short gasp, waiting for her ribs to crack.

What was that about? she wondered.

As Queenie recovered her breath, Iris ascended the spiral staircase to her bedroom. With each step, she discharged a slow windy release of gas, like a lonely train whistle fading in the distance. Iris glanced back at Queenie, as if determined to have the last word.

"Damn, voodoo curse," Iris said, a sigh escaping with the gas.

Hours later, before the sun rose on another steamy summer morning, Iris Temple finally did the one thing nobody in Savannah ever thought she would do. At the exact moment of Iris's departure, Queenie rolled over and smiled in her sleep. Meanwhile Spud Grainger startled awake with a sudden urge to play the saxophone.

The Mail Slot

The girl emerges from behind a hedge trimmed like a bad haircut which lines the sidewalk across the street and partially hides the house where she lives. She looks both ways before crossing the street, and then opens the squeaky iron gate in front of Allison Whitworth's house.

Allison observes the girl through curtains open the width of a tightly woven cocoon, clutches the top of her sweater and steps into the shadows of the grandfather clock in the entryway. She smells the lemon-scented furniture oil she'd applied to the clock cabinet the day before.

Go away, Allison wants to tell her. *Leave me alone.*

Why is she here anyway? Is it that time of year again? The time for endless school fundraisers, the selling of Girl Scout cookies and tickets for raffles? What would someone like Allison do with a Jamaican cruise, a Florida vacation? Has the girl forgotten that every year she knocks and every year there is no answer?

The knock quiets Allison's thoughts, a rapping so timid she reaches toward the crystal doorknob before withdrawing her hand. Her heartbeat accelerates. Her breathing grows shallow; her hands clammy. She forces herself to take deep breaths.

The knock comes again, this time a little stronger. The girl waits. She stands not three feet away from Allison and opens the brass mail slot in the center of the wooden door with her index finger.

"I know you're in there," she whispers through the opening. "There's nothing to be afraid of. I want to be your friend."

Allison shuffles backward, touching the cool wall with one hand while covering her mouth with the other. Her throat grows tight, as if to stifle any words that might escape. How many years has it been since she had a friend? Maybe since St. Marks, the school she attended until her father suddenly died of a heart attack, and before her mother's lengthy illness. Mary McMurray was her best friend then. Her only friend.

The girl opens and closes the hinged flap.

"Why don't you talk to anybody?" she asks. "Why don't you ever come out of your house?"

Her questions drop through the slot like unwanted mail. The girl opens and closes the hinged flap three more times, as if to add question marks to her inquiry. She is close enough for Allison to hear her breathing.

"My name's Beth, short for Elizabeth," the girl begins again. "Elizabeth Fletcher Owens. The Fletcher part is my grandmother's name."

Allison bites her bottom lip and cautiously opens the curtains on the door's side panel. A thin, sunny slice of the girl appears. A dozen freckles are captured, one brown eye, and the corner of a blue barrette in the shape of a dolphin. The girl lets the mail flap close a final time and stands there for several seconds chewing thoughtfully on the end of her pony-tail. She turns to leave, bounding down the steps, looking back only once when she opens the gate.

Allison clutches the doorknob and turns it to open the door and call after the girl. She hesitates—her face hot—fear echoing in her ears. With a sigh, she releases her grip and gives the door two swift taps, as if double-locking the possibility of stepping outside.

To divert herself, Allison takes a monogrammed white handkerchief from the pocket of her skirt and blends in the smudge she made while leaning against the grandfather clock. She closes the slight opening in the curtains and walks over to the burgundy wingback chair that has stood in the same corner of the living room for as long as she can remember.

A rectangle of fading lace drapes across the chair back to protect the fabric. On Wednesdays, Allison takes her afternoon nap in this chair. She seldom sits on any piece of furniture twice in a week, in order to save on their wear. Because of this precaution, everything looks as it did when her parents were alive.

Allison's father grew up in this house, and Allison has lived here her entire life. In 1912, when the mansion had been built, this had been the most prestigious section of Atlanta. But in recent decades, newer, smaller houses have sprung up around her like weeds among rose bushes.

The grandfather clock ticks in the distance, a reticent reminder of time passing. It chimes on the hour as Allison settles into the large chair, her feet placed carefully on its matching ottoman. She doesn't remove her shoes, an act of defiance against her mother. The panty hose Allison wears gather at her ankles. She will add a new pair to her grocery list for her sister Melody; they don't seem to last long with all the cleaning she has to do.

Allison closes her eyes and rests into the sound of the grandfather clock. Her heartbeat returns to normal, though she can't stop thinking of the girl. Her breathing deepens. In her dreams she is a girl again. She sees herself walk to the dining room window and stands on her tiptoes to look outside. Children her age ride bicycles up and down the street, laughing and yelling at each other. Her mother does not allow Allison to play with them. She might get hurt. She might get dirty. She is a princess locked in a tower, waiting for one of them to notice her. The tall boy, perhaps. Henry. He was in her class at school the year before and always carried a baseball glove. In her mind she calls to Henry, willing him to see her, to break the spell and free her from the tower.

Scotty, Allison's cat, jumps in her lap and awakens her.

"Oh, Scotty," she says. "A perfect nap destroyed."

After she shoos him away she picks at several white hairs he left on her dark skirt. She secures them inside the right front pocket of her sweater vest and wonders why she puts up with him, though she already knows.

The cat looks at her, his tail swishing. She glances at her mother's gold wristwatch on her wrist. "It's not dinnertime yet," she says.

The cat jumps up again, forcing her to pet him. One day, two years before, he showed up at her back door, meowing as if he had simply come home for dinner. His insistence clouded her better judgment and she let him inside.

Allison named him after the school she always dreamed of attending, before her father's death had prevented such dreams. She was denied a college education because of lack of funds, though her sister, Melody, was still allowed to attend. Years later, after her mother died and their family attorney revealed the worth of the family estate, Allison nearly spit out the tea she was drinking: she could have attended any college in the world.

Allison smoothes the cat's whiskers. "Melody will be here soon," she tells him. "Of course, you aren't very fond of Melody, are you?" Allison smiles.

The day before, Allison spied the neighbor girl petting Scotty out on the sidewalk. Later, Scotty sat underneath the birdfeeder in the girl's side yard. Last evening he left a small dead wren framed in blood on the back porch stoop. Allison was so upset she yelled at him. It took several kettles of boiling water, poured carefully out the door at an awkward angle to remove the stain.

The backdoor slams. Melody calls from the kitchen. Allison walks stiffly into the room. More and more she has begun to feel her age, 67 now. Old but still fit; she never misses a single morning of her calisthenics. She believes they are responsible for her outliving her mother by twenty years and her father by twenty-five.

Her younger sister places two grocery bags on the kitchen counter. From the top of one of the bags Allison pulls out copies of this month's *Ladies Home Journal* and *Redbook* magazines. She finds these publications mundane, but reads them anyway. Occasionally she learns a helpful hint to remove a particular stain, or a new recipe for peach cobbler, her favorite dessert. But she would much more prefer *National Geographic* or *The New Yorker*.

Melody removes the usual things from the shopping bags. Allison's weekly menu varies little, except for occasional ingredients to make a cobbler if peaches are in season. Allison eyes the groceries to make sure Melody hasn't forgotten anything.

"You should eat different things sometimes," Melody says. "Variety is the spice of life, you know."

"I'm not like you," Allison says.

"That's true, you're not like me," Melody is quick to agree. "Jack and I had some friends over last weekend and we grilled salmon," she continues. "It's good to try new things."

Allison turns to hide her grimace. *I would sooner eat dandelions from the backyard than salmon*, she thinks.

On the second shelf of the cupboard, Allison places a small box of grits, her daily breakfast for as long as she can remember. Next to that, Allison stacks seven cans of tomato soup for the week, and aligns each label to face out. The remaining groceries are put away in their prescribed places. When finished, Allison smiles at her ordered creation like a child who has built an elaborate house of blocks. Wednesdays, when her cupboard is at its fullest, holds a satisfaction for Allison that few things do.

Melody studies her own reflection in the small mirror near the kitchen door. A casual observer would never guess the two were sisters. Besides their difference in age and height, Melody has the look of someone who goes to the country club for Sunday brunch: her clothes are perfectly tailored, her hair professionally colored to cover any gray. In contrast, Allison's hair is turning more gray every day, and she trims it herself when needed. She has worn the same outfits for twenty years; quality fabrics, built to last.

Melody retrieves a flat, square gift box from her ample purse and hands it to Allison. Inside is a light green scarf, the color of pea soup, a color Allison hates. "Hmm," she grunts, as if pleased, but wonders who she is supposed to impress with a fancy scarf.

Allison was twelve when Melody was born and long resigned to her status as an only child. They shared nothing in common except parents, both whom had become much more patient by the time Melody—a blond, curly-haired cherub—arrived. The result was a confidence Melody possesses and Allison envies.

"Do you need anything else?" Melody asks, checking her watch.

"No, I'm fine," Allison says, and in a way she is fine.

Even though she and her sister have never been close, Allison looks forward to Wednesdays, to Melody delivering her groceries. She puts on the teakettle to boil and places two aged porcelain teacups and saucers on the kitchen table. They are heirlooms from their English grandmother's tea set and are brought out only for special occasions.

Melody sits and emits a sigh, as if she hoped Allison had forgotten their ritual. She opens her purse and applies a fresh layer of lipstick that Allison realizes she will later be washing off the cup.

"Jack says we should talk about the house."

"Jack?" Allison asks, checking the flame's consistency beneath the water on the stove.

"You do remember Jack?" Melody asks, a touch of sarcasm in her voice. Ridicule was also their father's forte. He often teased Allison that she was *not worth a whit* as a Whitworth.

"Of course I remember Jack," Allison says, although at times she wished to forget him.

Whenever Jack comes to the house he runs his fingers over the antiques and picks up things on her father's desk, as if to determine their value. After he leaves Allison wipes off his fingerprints and opens the front windows to air out the smell of his stinking cigar.

"This old house is falling down around you, Allison. It needs repairs. We need to get workers in here." Melody sips the tea and leaves the lipstick signature. "At the very least it needs a new furnace."

"There's nothing wrong with the furnace," Allison replies, pulling her sweater close.

Her breathing goes shallow at the thought of workmen underfoot. They would track in dirt from the outside. It's hard to keep the house clean as it is. She forces herself to breathe deeply, remembering an article from *Redbook* that suggested this discipline when dealing with everyday anxiety.

"I can't stay long," Melody reminds her. She taps her artificial painted nails on the table that they used to sit at as girls.

As they sip tea together, Allison listens to the details of Melody's life—her volunteer work at the Methodist church, Jack's law practice, and her continual dissatisfaction with her friends. Melody is her own solar system. Allison nods, a willing captive in her orbit.

Later that night, while Allison stands at the kitchen sink washing the last of her dinner dishes, a familiar squeak announces the opening of the front gate. She quickly dries her hands and steps into the shadows of the entryway. It is the girl again. This time she doesn't knock or speak, but simply opens the mail slot and drops an envelope inside. Allison doesn't move. It is as if a grenade has dropped at her feet and the slightest breath might cause it to detonate. The girl crosses the street again and disappears behind the hedge.

Scotty circles the envelope and sniffs it before returning to his perch on the coffee table. Several ticks of the clock later, Allison carefully opens the letter. Inside is a note neatly printed on lined paper in the girl's handwriting:

Dear Miss Whitworth,

We are learning how to write personal letters in my class and for homework we are to write a letter to someone. I picked you. I hope you don't mind.

Sincerely,
Elizabeth Fletcher Owens

Below the girl's large cursive signature is a drawing of a cat.

Allison's face flushes. She can't remember the last time she received correspondence. Perhaps the last was from her Aunt Gwen, commending her on her unceasing devotion to her mother during her illness. Allison looks out the window again. Should she answer the girl?

Still flushed, Allison walks into the study and searches her father's desk for paper. In the bottom drawer she finds Whitworth stationary. She sits at the large roll-top desk and reaches for the fountain pen she uses to pay her bills. She writes in perfect script the words: *Dear Elizabeth Fletcher Owens.*

The open drawer, having once contained her father's cigars, still smells of sweet, pungent tobacco. The smell brings his memory into the room.

Don't encourage the girl, she hears him say. *What will she want next? You'll never get rid of her.*

Allison imagines an onslaught of Girl Scout cookies and raffle tickets descending on her and the girl knocking on the door at all hours. She crumples the piece of paper, walks into the kitchen and throws it in the trash.

"Yes, better to nip this in the bud," Allison says aloud.

Scotty stands at the kitchen door and meows his desire to go out again. Allison unlatches the dead bolt and opens the back door just enough for him to slip his slender body outside. Another gift that she'll have to clean up awaits her.

* * *

An unmarked white van is parked in front of the Whitworth house across the street. Old neighborhoods in Atlanta have a number of large gothic houses similar to this one, mixed in with smaller ranch styles like their own. As she did hundreds of times as a girl, Beth cuts through the hedge and crosses the street. A well-dressed older woman stands on the front porch. The same woman who visited the elder Miss Whitworth every week for as long as she can remember.

"I'm Beth Owens," she says, by way of introduction.

"Melody Whitworth." The woman offers a limp handshake.

"I'm home from college on spring break. Is everything okay?" Beth glances toward the van.

"My sister died in her sleep last night," the woman says, her eyes registering no grief. "The coroner was just here."

Beth leans against the porch railing, her knees weak. *How can the death of someone I've never even met have this effect?* she thinks.

Two men emerge from the house, each wearing black jackets and matching pants. A zippered black bag lay on the gurney between them, the remains of her neighbor for twenty years and a woman she's never seen. Balancing their load, they descend the porch steps and lift the body gently into the van. Beth watches them drive away, her gaze holding until the van turns the corner at the end of the street.

"The coroner said she died peacefully," Melody Whitworth says, as if this matters to her. She brushes a piece of chipped paint off the banister and narrows her eyes, perhaps making a mental note the house will need painting before sold. "Is there something I can help you with?" she adds.

"No, I was just a friend," Beth says.

Her eyebrows float above her glasses, as if doubting her sister had any friends.

"When I was younger I wrote her letters and put them in there." Beth points to the brass mail slot on the ornate wooden front door.

"Oh, you must be the little girl. Wait, I have something for you," she says, as she goes back inside.

While Beth waits, she remembers the first time she ventured onto this porch. Like that scene in *To Kill a Mockingbird* where Scout and Jem touch the door of Boo Radley's house, she dared herself to approach the old mansion. She isn't sure why she felt the need to liberate Miss Whitworth. Except back then she read a lot of stories about princesses locked in towers.

Melody Whitworth returns to the porch and places an elegant wooden box in Beth's hands that smells of lemon oil. "You should have these," she says.

Surprised by the heaviness of the box, Beth balances it on the porch railing in order to open it. Inside are stacks of her letters, circled with rubber bands, an index card marking each year.

"She kept them all?" Beth asks.

"They obviously meant a lot to her," she answers.

"I had no idea," Beth says.

The woman hesitates, as if deciding how much to share. "My sister had agoraphobia," she continues. "Doctors came to the house at first, but eventually they all gave up on her. She used to get out more when she was younger, but after our parents died. . . ." Her voice fades.

A heavy silence follows, as if their conversation has become agoraphobic, too.

"I'd catch her watching me sometimes, and I wanted to help somehow," Beth says. "To be honest, I think Miss Whitworth is why I decided to study psychology. I'm a junior at Agnes Scott," she continues. "I'm on scholarship. Otherwise my parents could never afford it."

"I imagine you've guessed who the anonymous donor was for your scholarship," Melody Whitworth says.

Beth pauses to make the connection. Why didn't she figure it out sooner? Her eyes mist.

"All this time I thought I rescued her, but it seems she rescued me," Beth says, her words soft.

Seconds later, Melody Whitworth pulls the front door closed and locks it with a key. She tests to make sure it is secure, the tarnished mail flap rocking on its hinges.

The End

To die would be an awfully big adventure. - J.M. Barrie

The evening starts with indigestion and ends with me floating near the ceiling looking down at my body in the bed.

This must be what they call an out-of-body experience, I say with a chuckle. As a Southern Baptist, I always hated those New Age nuts.

My wife Abby shakes me and cries: "Don't you dare do this to me!"

While on the phone to 911 she stops crying long enough to take my wrist and search for my pulse. When she can't find one, she starts crying again.

The last time she bawled like this was when our dog Loretta died. She loved that mutt. At the time I remember thinking: *I hope she grieves this much for me when I'm pushing up daisies.* I guess that's exactly what's happened. I am gone. A daisy pusher. Just like Loretta. Except Loretta got cancer and for months we took her into the vet for chemo even though it didn't do any good. I think we tortured old Loretta at the end, when we should have just let her go. But there's no problem letting go this time, at least not on my end. No blaze. No glory. No prolonged goodbyes. No goodbye at all.

What's weird is that I can still see and hear things—the end of my life playing out like a movie on Netflix streaming, with only a two-star review. Then our two Springer spaniels, Wynonna and Naomi, bark and sing like they always do at sirens. When an EMS van pulls in front of our house, Abby lets the dogs out into the fenced backyard so they won't jump all over the two paramedics, a man and a woman, who look like they've been up all night drinking double espressos.

The young woman—our daughter's age—takes my wife into the hallway and tells her that they'll do everything they can, but her job is to stay calm. Abby has never been calm a minute of her life. I have the therapy bills to prove it. So I'm not sure it will work, but it's a nice thought.

Still hovering in the corner, I say: *Sweet Jesus, am I really dead? I'm only fifty. Prime of life, for Christ's sake.* Then I look around to see if I've taken His name in vain. But nobody seems to be keeping track of sins or calling roll in the clouds and there's no white light to walk toward. No sunset to fade into, either. Instead, it's like those dreams where you show up to an empty classroom and realize you've missed the final exam of a class you forgot to attend.

Can we rewrite this scene? I say to the guy in charge, but there is no response.

The other paramedic has acne and a vine tattooed around his wrist, the initials *J.C.* intertwined with the leaves. After taking out a stethoscope, he listens to my chest and then puts two fingers on my neck before he rips open my pajamas.

"Why don't you guys ever exercise?" he says to me.

Before I have time to explain how busy I am at work and how the bad back doesn't help, he takes out those paddles you see on television and turns up the voltage and says, "Clear," even though there's nobody in the room except him and me.

After the jolt, nothing happens, but he does it again and then again, like he's thinking *third time's the charm.* Then he whispers, *fuck*, like he really hoped it would work.

My wife turns on the waterworks again, but I can't take my eyes off the man in the bed with the big belly who has suddenly gone belly up. Needless to say, if I'd known my existence would deep six at four in the morning, two weeks after my 50th birthday party, I might have done some things differently, like actually taken care of myself.

We threw a big bash out in the backyard for friends and family from all over the country. I made my famous barbeque ribs with all the fixin's and we had a keg of beer. Everybody wore black, and dozens of black balloons were tied to the deck. Then our three grown kids arrived driving an old hearse—as a joke, of course—complete with an empty coffin in the back and my youngest son dressed as the grim reaper.

Oh, God, the kids are never going to forgive me for this. They've been on me for years to quit smoking and lose weight. But I couldn't imagine a life without a cold Bud and fried chicken with milk gravy like my mama used to make.

Meanwhile, I'm wearing the pajamas my wife gave me for Christmas last year with *Papa Bear* monogrammed in red on the front. I remember thinking when I opened the present that I wouldn't want to be caught dead in these pajamas and here I am. Dead. Curtains for *Papa Bear*, who has cashed in his chips and bought a farm in Tennessee he never wanted. All the while hoping for another chance at life, because it's way too soon to roll the credits.

Gullah Secrets

The land is living. The waterways and marshland along the South Carolina coast are living. The oak trees are living. For me, everything I touch, everything I encounter is alive. Even my Gullah ancestors, who some would say have gone out with the tide of time, remain present, and speak to me. The Gullah spells are as much a part of me as the breath that fills my lungs. To protect the people I love from bad things that might happen to them, I mix potions. For some time now, I've been getting the message that an ill wind is blowing in. I'm not sure when. I'm not sure how. But something is coming. The tea leaves show it. The wind whispers it. The voice of my ancestors confirms it, and I will get ready for it the best I can.

The Gullah ways were taught to me by my grandmother, Sadie, a slave for the Temple family of Savannah. Today, I still work for this same family as their maid, housekeeper and nanny. For forty years I've worked for the current Temples. Iris Temple and Mister Oscar have two children: Edward, nearly grown and away at boarding schools most of the year, and Rose, ten years of age, handed over to my care when she was but minutes old.

Somewhere around the age of sixty, 'old' was added to my name and I've never complained. I'll hear: "Old Sally, go and fetch the newspaper for me." Or "Old Sally, get that child out of my sight."

Some days I feel older than my years, having worked as a housekeeper all my life and raised three children of my own. My youngest, Ivy, still lives with me, even though she's in her twenties now.

Although the Temples reside in downtown Savannah, I live twenty miles north on the South Carolina coast on land that my grandmother and mother owned before me. It is a place where Atlantic tides bathe the islands and coastland, where waterways work inland into pungent marshes, now home to shrimp and crab. Oysters grow in slick, gray colonies like necklaces along the scooped neck of the land. Osprey and cranes patrol the salt waters. Sea gulls squawk and hover above shrimp boats heading out to sea. Spanish moss graces live oaks like long silver earrings dangling on the ears of a beautiful woman. Coastal winters run chilly to mild, summers sticky to steamy.

My ancestors wove sweet-grass baskets. They made medicine of herbs and grew all their own food. When it came time to give birth, they delivered their own babies. They reaped the bounty of surrounding waters with fishing nets they knitted themselves. They lived off ocean and land with peaceful self-reliance. Yet that peace feels threatened now.

Today, I am grateful the Temples are traveling so I can bring the girls to my house on the beach. So as not to get behind, I take my ironing with me. In the kitchen, I refill a coke bottle with water and twist a metal cap on the top so I can sprinkle the sheets before ironing them. A portrait of Dr. Martin Luther King, Jr. shares a wall with photos of my children, grandchildren and great grandchildren.

I stir roots boiling on the stove, the water already black as the swamps where I collect them. I am conjuring up a new batch of protection spell for Rose. Protection spells were my mama's specialty. She lived past the age of 90 as an independent woman, still chopping her own firewood, washing clothes in a tin tub and cooking on a cast-iron stove.

Through the large windows of my small house facing the sea, I keep an eye on the two children in my charge while they build a sand castle on the beach. One is brown, the other one white; one older and one younger.

Violet, the youngest girl, is six years old and the most beautiful child I have ever seen. She's my granddaughter, who I have agreed to raise. It's in my nature to raise up whoever needs rearing. It doesn't matter if they are my own blood or not.

Earlier that morning, I wove Violet's hair into several braids and added colored beads to the end of the tight rows. Despite her circumstances of coming into this world, Violet is a happy child. She often sings or hums, the beads in her braids keeping the beat as she moves her head with the melody. She makes up most of her songs. Often I'll find her with her eyes closed, feet stomping and hands clapping as she sways with the music. It's as if someone much older and wiser resides within her. Someone who has stories to tell.

Rose Temple, on the other hand, holds her music deep inside. If I live to be a hundred, I will never understand how somebody like Iris Temple—Rose's mother—given so much in this world, can be so stingy with her love. It's as though the ancestral line of Temple women suffered a drought of feeling that changed the landscape from the lush low country marsh into a desert. Time and again, Rose clings to me like I am the oasis she seeks.

Ivy, my grown daughter, her waist and hips already thick with good eating, helps the girls carry bucket loads of sea water to fill the moat around their sand castle. In many ways Ivy still seems like a girl herself, though grownup things have happened to her.

After turning off the roots boiling on the stove, I make egg salad sandwiches and sweet tea. I wave from the front porch, calling the girls to lunch. It is spring and the blowing sea breeze provides the perfect temperature. Something sweet is in the air; something blooming in the dunes. I close my eyes to identify the scent but it is gone before I can catch it. Dark clouds push in on my thoughts.

The girls run through the dunes and up the steps to my small beach house painted white with bright blue trim to scare off evil spirits. The girls are covered with sand. Ivy follows, her sleeveless cotton dress blowing in the breeze as she brushes sand off her brown arms and legs.

"Ivy, please wash off the girls before they come inside," I say. "I don't want to have to sweep again today."

"Yes, mama." Ivy grabs the green garden hose at the side of the house and rinses the sand off their arms and legs. The girls squeal in ecstasy as Ivy covers the end of the hose with her thumb and sends water spraying in all directions.

I return to my ironing. If I hurry I can get one more piece done before lunch. The sound of laughter makes me wonder if I've imagined the omens. But the truth nags at me like a headache that refuses to go away.

The two girls wrap themselves in clean towels hanging on the porch railings and come into the living room where I am ironing my fourth full sheet of the day. Only four more to go. I shake the sprinkler bottle across the wrinkled sheet. My iron sizzles as it hits the damp cloth. Steam rises. Sweat dots my brow.

Rose leans into my wide hip. Birthing hips, I call them; perfect for bringing children into the world. With my hand, I smooth Rose's wet hair and notice again how thin she is.

"I've got to fatten you up, child."

Yet Rose could eat chicken and dumplings every day of her life and stay skinny. She's tall for her age, too, most all legs. Her mother keeps her hair styled and permed like a prize-winning poodle and Rose is always tugging at it to make it straight. I lean over and kiss her forehead, marking her with my love.

"Baptize me," Rose says. She stands as tall as my shoulder and looks up at me, her eyes filled with playful pleading. She asks me to do this every time I iron, as if this is the food she needs most.

After I agree, Rose turns toward the sea and bows her head as though about to receive a sacred anointment. The water sprinkles on Rose's head, and her laughter rides on the salty breeze sweeping through the house.

Violet begs to be next and I repeat my christening ritual. Then Violet and Rose collapse in giggles on the sofa. Ivy shakes her head, as if she is much too old for such nonsense, so I aim a few sprinkles in her direction. My daughter, who also seems much too serious these days, laughs a little.

The four of us move to the kitchen where I have already set out their lunch on my round wooden table. The girls and Ivy eat egg salad sandwiches cut into triangles like the finger sandwiches served at Iris Temple's fancy parties. Slices of watermelon are piled high on a plate in the middle of the table and they devour these, too, collecting all the seeds in a bowl for me to plant. The thirsty girls drink glass after glass of sweet tea with a slice of lemon perched on the lip of each glass. Meanwhile, I reheat shrimp and grits from my dinner the night before and join them.

"What's that smell?" Rose asks. She wipes her mouth with a napkin as if her mother might be watching.

"That be something I'm conjuring up." I push back my chair and walk to the stove, my bad hip already stiff from a few moments sitting. With a wooden spoon, I give the root mixture a stir and then spread the roots on towels laid out on the kitchen counter. I pour the black brew into a brown bottle with a stopper. This mixture is stronger than my usual potions because what I'm guarding against seems to require it.

On the Sea Islands—those islands and coastal regions along the Georgia and South Carolina coast—magical medicines are created using feathers, bones, and sometimes blood, fingernails and hair clippings. These oddities will then be mixed with more natural materials such as roots, sand and leaves. Since the white slave owners feared the use of Gullah magic, conjuring practices were kept hidden and are held secret even today. I've not used one of the old spells in a long time, but whatever is coming feels very old.

"Grandma's spells get rid of evil spirits," Violet says to Rose, her eyes widening as she says 'evil spirits.' She shakes her head to get her beaded braids to agree and the girls giggle again.

I retrieve a Saltine cracker tin filled with homemade oatmeal cookies from the cabinet, and give the girls two each and Ivy three. Ivy wraps her cookies in a napkin and puts them in her dress pocket.

Violet carries her plate and glass to the sink and Rose follows. Though younger, Violet is always the leader.

"Can we go back out?" Violet asks me. "We still have work to do." The girls exchange a look as if their 'work' is of the top-secret variety.

I nod. Violet challenges Rose to a race, the finish line being their sandcastles. It is inevitable that Violet will lose. She is a foot shorter than Rose and three years younger. Yet the two girls toss their towels across the porch railing and make a mad dash through the dunes as if equally paired.

Ivy and I reach the porch just as Rose throws up her arms in victory in the distance. Violet lags far behind swinging her head as she runs, as if enjoying the sound of the beads swaying in her hair and happy to let Rose win.

"I'm glad we came out today," Ivy says.

"Me, too," I say. "I much prefer the sea breezes to that stuffy old Temple house."

Ivy drove us to the coast since I never learned to drive. Mister Oscar, Miss Temple's husband, is good about letting Ivy use one of their cars if needed. He holds a fondness for Ivy that we never talk about.

Ivy and I sit on the top step looking out over the Atlantic Ocean. The sun is just beyond the house and the porch is in shadows now. It feels good to rest a bit before starting on the ironing again. Violet and Rose begin to build a new sandcastle next to the old one. If not for the differences in the color of their skin, they might pass as sisters.

"They call themselves the sea gypsies," Ivy says. "It's their secret society for girls."

I laugh. "Imagination. It be a powerful thing."

"They've appointed me their queen," Ivy says, rolling her eyes.

I put an arm around Ivy and squeeze a dose of love into her. "You be a queen to me, too."

Ivy lowers her head. Her hair is clipped short, and to tame it she wears colorful headbands I make from fabric I find. Today's band is bright yellow, the color of a shiny ripe lemon. Ivy has always liked bold colors. The bolder the better. I give her another squeeze, pretending I'm making lemonade.

"So what be on your mind, baby?" I ask. "Not like you to be so quiet."

Ivy's brow furrows, as if whatever she's pondering has steered her into deep waters she's not sure she can navigate.

"I need to make a decision, Mama. Mister Oscar wants me to move into the house and be Iris's companion."

Now I am the quiet one. I'm certain Mister Oscar has other reasons for wanting Ivy there. Bad omens creak through my bones. Then the words come out of my mouth before I have time to stop them:

"You have to make a living some way, baby, and since he be offering room and board…" My voice trails off.

Ivy huffs and jerks away. No one in their right mind would want to be a companion to Iris Temple. I can barely stand working for her, myself. But Ivy hasn't found steady work yet, and I barely make enough to support Ivy, Violet and myself.

Silence stretches in front of us like the yawning beach along the coastline. I hang my head. Though it is steamy hot, I shiver. I always swore I would never do to my daughter what my mother did to me. But here I've done it anyway. In contrast to the stormy feelings churning inside me, the ocean is so calm it looks like a sheet of dark blue glass.

Ivy has tears in her eyes, but isn't making a sound. I search for words to say. Then I take a deep breath and my voice comes out soft, "Daughter, sometimes history and the times be bigger than a single person," I begin. "And I think this be one of those times. I don't know how to tell you to do anything different than what I did with my own life. I wish it weren't so, but it is."

Ivy is the daughter of Iris Temple's father. The fact that she has a different father than her brothers has never been a secret to Ivy. Edward Temple was a powerful man. A man used to getting whatever he wanted, including me. No love involved. I needed my job because I had a family to support.

Children fathered by landowners and servants was not that unusual in those days and in some ways the old days are still going on. Temple blood has been mixing with my ancestors for centuries now. My grandmother, Sadie, carried and raised a Temple child, too, and now Mister Oscar has made his choice and wants Ivy.

For days, I have mixed an elixir to ward off the darkness I thought was coming from somewhere far away, but instead it lurked in my own bloodline. It doesn't matter that I was the first in my family to finish high school, and that I harbor a room full of books that I've read, or that I know a hundred potions I can create. Sometimes the surge of history just runs too deep and too strong. Sometimes no matter how much you learn to read the ocean currents, you still get swept into the undertow.

Rose and Violet run up to the porch and collapse smiling into my arms. Their embrace is warm, sandy and sprinkled with sunlight. The delight of the two girls pulls me away from the past and back into the present moment. A new wave of certainty surges through me stronger than the undercurrent. Even though it looks like history is circling back to repeat itself with Ivy, something else is true, too. Change is coming. I'm not sure when. I'm not sure how. But it is coming as surely as the sun promises to rise tomorrow morning.

Country Obituary - #1

Cecil "Bluebird" Crawford died peacefully in his sleep early Sunday morning, December 7, 2014. He was 102 years old, which is not nearly old enough. Cause of death is oldness.

He was born in Jacob's Ridge and spent his entire life here except for 3 years in the Army fighting the Germans in World War II. He built houses, starting with big ones—all of which are still standing and some of you are living in—and ending with small ones, bird houses that are perched on porches and in trees all over the county, all gifts from Bluebird.

He is survived by his wife of eighty years, Margaret Annabeth Holston Crawford, ("Maggie") who he met in elementary school in the cafeteria line and they'd been friends ever since. He also leaves behind his daughters Muriel and Mary Beth and the twins: Cecil, Jr. "Junior" and Bill "Bubba" (Bubba preceded him to the Hereafter).

Grandchildren left behind are Brian, Cecil Jr., and Cynthia Winston; Kathryn Jensen Wyatt and Annabeth Mulberry. Tinker and Tucker Crawford; Elizabeth, Fran and Mitsy Crawford. (Mitsy died of cancer three years ago.) Great-grandchildren are Thomas, Chase, Jessica, Sheila, Abigail, Trevor and Roy-boy. Great-greats are Caleb and Harper (twins again) who he rocked in his lap the afternoon before he died.

Services will be held at Good River Baptist Church at 3 p.m. on Saturday, giving the family time to get here, as they are scattered all across the country.

Cards and letters of condolence can be sent to Maggie Crawford, # 7 County Rd., Jacob's Ridge, NC.

Bluebird will be remembered by everyone who knew him. For over forty years he drove the tractor pulling the Knights of Columbus float during our annual Christmas parade, and for the last twenty years he played Santa. Except for the extra padding needed, he bore a striking resemblance. He also had a beautiful tenor voice that could bring tears to your eyes, and that the Good River Baptist Church Choir will surely miss.

As one of the best bird-callers in the State of North Carolina, he could imitate not only southern birds, but also some of the ones that just passed through on their way to somewhere else. However, he will mostly be remembered for his walks along the river every day of his life—a familiar sight, rain or shine—up until the day he died.

Bluebird had a smile and a kind word for everybody and if anybody ever needed anything, he was on your porch the next day delivering it. He said the hardest thing about growing old was seeing his friends go on before him, but he never complained a minute of his life. Bluebird was a true southern gentleman, and the world is a little less gentle without him in it. Be sure and get to the church early because there's bound to be a crowd.

Country Obituary - #2

Margaret Annabeth Holston Crawford, passed away late yesterday afternoon, March 15, 2015, three months after losing her beloved husband, Cecil "Bluebird" Crawford. She was 99 years of age. Cause of death is heart attack, but we all know it broke her heart when Bluebird died.

Known as "Maggie" to family and friends, Maggie Crawford taught school at Jacob's Ridge Elementary for forty years. A bunch of you probably had her in third grade and have beautiful cursive handwriting as a result. After she retired, Maggie volunteered for the adult literacy program, and was a founding member of the Jacob's Ridge Garden Club. Members of the Good River Baptist Church will remember her for the delicious candied yams and apple pies she brought to the potlucks.

She is survived by her daughters Muriel and Mary Beth, and one of the twins: Cecil, Jr. "Junior." The other twin, Bill "Bubba" Crawford preceded her in death.

Grandchildren left behind are Brian, Cecil Jr., and Cynthia Winston; Kathryn Jensen Wyatt and Annabeth Mulberry. Tinker and Tucker Crawford; Elizabeth, Fran and Mitsy Crawford (Mitsy is also deceased). Great-grandchildren are Thomas, Chase, Jessica, Sheila, Abigail, Trevor and Roy-boy.

Great-greats are Caleb and Harper (twins), as well as newborn great-great grandson, Chester Cecil Wyatt.

Services will be held at Good River Baptist Church at 4 p.m. on Sunday, giving the family time to return from their homes in California, Illinois and Missouri.

Maggie could be shy, especially when compared to Bluebird, but will be remembered most for her contagious laugh. Bluebird had a knack for getting her started and many a choir practice was spent with Bluebird saying something funny and Maggie—in the middle of the altos—starting to laugh, until the entire choir was in stitches or running to the bathroom!

Maggie had one of the most beautiful flower gardens in Jacob's Ridge and for years her house was on the garden tour. She also dressed up as Mrs. Claus when Bluebird played Santa. But mostly she will be remembered as being a loving teacher, mother, grandmother, great grandmother, and great-great grandmother. Family, friends and former students, many of whom she kept in touch with, will miss her mightily.

Maggie will be laid to rest in the Good River Baptist Church Cemetery, on the hillside under the giant oak, right next to Bluebird.

River Reunion

The seven of us met at the trial and had dinner together the day the verdict came in. Guilty. Jeremy K. Watson was guilty. Not that anyone had to tell us that.

Although we lived all over the country, we decided to come together every year on the same day. For thirty years now we've met at my cabin in the mountains of North Carolina. It's nothing fancy, but with 30 acres, it's a private mountain retreat.

The first year we met at my cabin we took a group photograph on the front porch. Later we realized we looked so much alike we could have been sisters. Jeremy K. Watson had a type of woman he chose. All of us had been blonde at one time and wore our hair long. We were around the same height—five feet, seven inches. Selected because we represented someone, not because we did anything wrong. Or believed something he didn't like. Our crime was to look a certain way and to live alone.

Four of us remain, all in our seventies now. Tonight the moon is full and the sky filled with stars. We walk the path to the open field by the river where I laid a fire earlier that afternoon. On our first weekend together, all those many years ago, we had simply built a fire and sat around it talking. Comparing stories. Listening. The talking cure. Then, over the years, we leaned on each other when life got rough, encouraging each other to move beyond merely surviving.

In her travels, Julie—a retired counselor—visited various healers and brought back rituals. One year we burned anything we wanted to get rid of in our lives. Toxic reminders of the past, of which we had plenty. Another year we drummed on various makeshift drums, releasing our prayers to heaven. Another year we danced around the fire. All but me joined in. I have been slow to trust these women, and slower still to trust myself.

This year, Julie leads us in a ceremony where we cover our faces with the black charcoals left from previous fires. As with everything she suggests, I am skeptical. We pass the spent wood, as light as a charcoal pencil, and use it to paint our faces. Within minutes, we are covered in darkness, only the whites of our eyes and our teeth are visible. I have never liked getting dirty, but we giggle at the sight of each other, as if going from white to dark as night is something magical.

The stars call down to us tonight. Ursula Major, the Little Dipper, Orion's Belt. Venus winks at us, as well.

"Isn't there a Native American story where all the fallen warriors return to the sky?" I ask. I remember reading it to the fourth graders I used to teach.

"If that's true, we've got entire tribes watching over us," Maggie says.

"Can't women be warriors, too?" Claire asks.

The fire crackles in agreement.

"We're the warriors," Julie says. "We refused to be defeated."

"I like that," Claire says. The others agree. In truth, Claire looks the least warrior-like of all of us.

We sit on logs surrounding the fire pit. Seven originally, but now three spaces are empty until I place Jane's ashes on one of them. It was Jane's final request that her ashes be released on the river, and her husband sent them by UPS. We plan to release them tomorrow morning. Meanwhile, the white square box that holds the remains of our friend looks like an order of Chinese takeout. Takeout illuminated by the moon. Claire takes a piece of charcoal and blacks out the box. No one speaks as we watch the last bit of white disappear.

Four women surround the fire. Four women and a box containing the ashes of the fifth. We look like part of a Lenten ceremony that got out of hand. I think of the women missing from this circle. Shirley went first, four or five years after our first meeting, and then Maryann about ten years ago and now Jane. Last year, Jane was so weak from chemo we all guessed that she wouldn't be with us this year. Yet the reality of it is difficult to face.

Claire begins to sing, her lilting voice sounding like someone much younger. I remember the year we discovered she could sing. An angel was among us disguised as a grandmother. That night Claire told us she had once lived in New

York City and had sung in several off-Broadway productions. After she was attacked, she stopped singing until two years ago, when she suddenly felt like singing again at one of our reunions.

Nobody is as they seem, I remind myself. Rich talents hide in unlikely people.

The song Claire sings has no words, yet the melody arches toward the moon. It moves into a minor key, as life does sometimes for many of us. The melody now is harrowing, sad. A lullaby where the baby and bough are dropped, cradle and all.

Women who have been victims of violent crime often feel betrayed by life, as if an Eternal Mother somehow dropped us and abandoned us to die. Yet, over the years, we have found our way back to the Mother: back to Nature, the one thing we are convinced can heal the deepest of wounds.

When the singing stops, Maggie pulls a long, slender joint from her skirt pocket. "I brought something for us," she says.

Wine is usually our drug of choice, but no one complains. We watch as Maggie lights it with a stick from the fire. I wonder how long it's been since I had a joint. The late eighties?

"A gift from the earth," she says, inhaling deeply. Maggie is an artist.

We pass the joint, as if passing a communion chalice.

"Don't tell my grandchildren about this," Claire says. "I wouldn't want to give them the wrong idea." She holds her breath in and then begins to sing again after she exhales the smoke.

Maggie sways to the music and rises to dance. She is the most free-spirited in our group, the least inhibited, while I am the most. Maggie weaves in between us as Claire sings her haunting melody. It was hot today, almost ninety, and humidity hangs thick in the air.

Sliding off her shorts and unbuttoning her oxford shirt, it is Julie who begins to take her clothes off first, as if undressing to ready herself for bed. She flings her clothes into the darkness. I gasp, and then giggle. Her white, wrinkled skin mixed with the charcoal makes her look like a creature who is half woman, half zebra.

"I wasn't a bra burner in the sixties, but I am now." Julie laughs and tosses her bra and panties into the fire. We all laugh with her. We are way past middle age, but feeling our youth.

After Maggie cheers her on, she unbuttons her own blouse and slips it off, along with her skirt. The joint passes to me. I inhale deeply, hoping to take in the courage the others have. Claire's song evolves into a stream of giggles, like the evening has called for a release and laughter is the current we ride to get there. Now totally naked, Maggie continues to dance. I cover my eyes, until I realize no one else is embarrassed. Especially not Maggie.

Now Claire takes off her clothes and flings them into the trees. Maggie hoots. Julie howls. The full moon watches us.

"Sing more," I say to Claire. I want her to never stop, but it is she who gets naked now, her plump body the whitest of all. She takes the cold coals at the edge of the fire and spreads the night over her skin. Maggie and Julie help to cover her.

I take another deep inhale of the joint and pass it on. It is my turn now, but I've never made peace with my naked body and the scars Jeremy K. Watson left behind.

How brave they are, these women in their seventies, baring body and soul, showing up in our small circle in their birthday suits. Vulnerable and flawed. Wrinkles, like tree rings, showing the number of seasons they've survived. Wrinkles that need to be celebrated, not judged. Wrinkles that Jane is no longer privileged to have. Aging is a privilege, not a birthright.

At least I am alive, I tell myself, *even if I am a coward.*

The naked women dance around the fire. The only one clothed, my shame anchors me to the log where I sit. Maggie dances close and pulls me gently toward standing. Her eyes search mine. They plead. They understand. They invite me to join them. The fire crackles as if amused by my plight. I am frozen in the warm night. Iced over. A queen of ice, with no idea of how to thaw. The marijuana blurs the scene. Will I remember any of this tomorrow morning? Or maybe this is all a dream. I want to let go. But let go of what?

Your resistance, the fire says. *Let yourself burn like me.*

Oh great, I say to myself, *hallucinations have started.* Is it time to finally release the burden I've carried for nearly forty years?

The night pulses with energy. A forest of animals watch the wildness of these human crones. Dancing crones. Claiming what is finally ours. The moon's wisdom. The night's secrets. Julie's burnt bra clings to the fire like a charred question mark. What am I to do now? What if I can't let go? But I want to. I want to.

Maggie continues to dance to an inner melody. She kisses me softly on the lips. A kiss for the frozen princess to startle her awake. I haven't been kissed for years. Not even briefly like this, and with such soft lips. Then Claire comes and then Julie. While Maggie kisses my cheeks and forehead, Julie unbuttons my shirt. They each take a sleeve of my blouse and coax the fabric down my arms. Claire begins to sing again while my heart beats like jungle drums. Then I step out of my jeans. Even in summer I wear pants and long sleeves to cover the scars. The shedding of clothes makes me feel light. Unencumbered. The air kisses my skin, like the invisible spider webs that cover the morning trail that I walk through to christen a new day.

Eyes closed, the marijuana helps me let go. I feel exposed, yet also safe. I know these women will not shame me. In the darkness I stand in my underwear.

Old lady underwear, I call it. Roomy and white.

But I don't feel like an old lady now. I am a girl in old skin. My face grows hot with the awareness that even in the moonlight the women can see the biggest scar. A knife aimed at my heart that somehow missed. An angel's breath of a distance between life and death.

Someone kisses the scar and ice melts along with the shame. I move as though blown by a gentle breeze. The fire warms my already warm skin. Eyes open now, I toss bra and panties onto the fire. A wide smile feels strange to my face. Smoke rises before the flame takes them, the mountains in shadow around us. In the distance, the river calls me. We are all connected. The women, the fire, the moon, the river, and every creature that lives here.

"Let's go skinny-dipping," Julie suggests.

The idea ignites us. As one unit, we grab flashlights and move toward the river.

"Wait," I say. I run back to get Jane's ashes, tucking the box under my arm before joining up with the group again.

A thousand yards away is the swimming hole where I swim every morning from spring to fall. We have swum here together before, but we always wore bathing suits and it was during the day. Never at night. Never feeling this free.

At first, seeing the bare bodies of my friends was shocking, but I am getting used to them now. The roundness of one, the slenderness of another, the drooping of breasts and skin as gravity pulls us toward our final resting places. The beautiful bodies that have seen us through so much.

Since I know the land best, I lead the way. We are naked, except for shoes, our flashlights bobbing in the darkness. Moonlight splashes across the path making its way through the canopy of trees. The sound of the river reaches for us, the most soothing sound on earth, next to the ocean. I think again how grateful I am that I live here in the mountains next to a river. A glorified mountain stream, really. That's all it is. Yet someone named it a river and the name stuck.

A small animal scurries along the path in front of us, and we scream like we are girls again.

"It's just a mother possum," I say, shining my flashlight on the silver body scurrying away. Possum's are ugly, yet they are good mothers. Like all of us, she is trying to live the life she was meant to live.

Claire shudders and says the possum reminds her of Jeremy K. Watson. We scream again, and then laugh, as if the spell he has had over us for decades is finally broken. The crickets celebrate and turn up their song.

At the edge of the swimming hole, we take off our shoes and wade into the dark water. I leave Jane's ashes sitting next to my sneakers in a spot of moonlight coming through the beech trees.

She can watch from here, I think.

Beech trees grow next to the river. At one time they were believed to be royalty—queens of the forest, while oaks were the kings. If that is true, the four of us are surrounded by queens and kings, a royal court with princes and princesses growing in the shadows of their parents.

For a second, I see something in the darkness. A ghost perhaps, for there are ghosts here. Has Jeremy K. Watkins returned? But then the fear fades and is washed down the river, and I am left with a soft serenity.

The water is chilly at first and then perfect. We giggle and float, the water washing the soot and ash from our bodies. The moonlight dances on the water and the night turns up its magic. We talk about Jane and Maryann and Shirley—those who are no longer with us—and wish them a peaceful rest. Then we become quiet ourselves.

The water holds me, and I feel myself relax. Tears pool in my eyes, the moon blurring overhead. My breathing deepens into an awareness that surprises me: I could die in this moment and feel content, knowing I have completed everything life required of me. I have even been brave.

Tears fall and return to the river. Tears that will eventually return to the sea. It is the quietest night on earth. A moment more sacred than any I've ever experienced in a church. My cathedral now is an unroofed one, the sanctuary filled with the entire night sky. As queens and kings witness the long-awaited ceremony, I am whole, newly born of the river.

Scarlett and Rhett Redux

An elderly couple approaches pushing a baby stroller, perhaps taking a grandchild or a great grand for a walk, a scene reminiscent of the St. Augustine of my childhood, forty years before.

North Florida boasts a year-round mild climate perfect for strolling the historic district, with its cobblestone streets, quaint cafes, unique shops and bed-and-breakfast inns. I am visiting my parents who own one of those quaint cafes. However, apart from visiting them, I also relish the opportunity to get away from big city life for a while and escape to a town with fewer crackpots.

We exchange greetings and pleasantries about the weather, which is indeed pleasant. Meanwhile, the couple reminds me of an upscale version of my grandparents.

Although I'm not an expert on babies or strollers, the push carriage boasts an impressive design. In the traditional English style with a chromium plated chassis, it also has stylish chrome and white wheels whose spokes sparkle in the sunlight. A ride befitting royalty. Enclosing the fortunate passenger, is a refined privacy curtain in delicate light blue organza.

When I lean over with a smile to offer the expected *oohs* and *ahhs*, shrill barks ensue, causing me to mutter profanities and take a rapid step back while clutching a tall skinny latte to my chest.

"Scarlett is frightened of strangers," the elderly woman says.

"And Rhett doesn't give a damn," the gentleman chuckles with a smile.

He lifts the privacy curtain to reveal two small dogs—the kind Paris Hilton might sport—that look like blonde rats. Scarlett and Rhett wear costumes. Scarlett a little tutu—pink—with ruffled lace, and Rhett, a simple black bow tie befitting a tux.

As I step closer, Scarlett lunges with a high-pitched growl toward my crotch.

"Whoa, there," I say, and position a protective hand over the zipper of my khakis. From the side, I think I see Rhett smile.

Scarlett's small chest heaves her excitement, as Rhett begins to lick his private parts with the dexterity of a Cirque du Soleil performer.

"Rhett, darling, where are your manners?" The woman places a polished fingernail under his chin and scratches.

While Rhett receives this attention, Scarlett pouts and pushes her tutu into Rhett's face. With a snorting gasp, Rhett renews his quest for the family jewels.

Am I on one of those television programs where hidden cameras film unsuspecting chumps? I wonder.

Flashing a smile toward a cluster of nearby palm trees, I suck in my gut and offer by best profile. Scarlett is not impressed.

"Do you have dogs?" the woman asks.

"Not anymore," I say. "Did when I was a boy, of course, but Duke was a German shepherd." *And could have eaten these blonde rats for breakfast,* I want to say.

The tutu still in Rhett's face, he lets out his first growl, as though he's heard my thought. Then Scarlett lets out a whimper that could turn the head of any male.

"You two behave," the older gentleman says.

Since television crews have not arrived, I now ponder what might have happened to cause this seemingly normal couple to transfer all their affection onto two dogs. Did they lose two infants in some devastating tragedy? Perhaps while *Gone with the Wind* played at the local theater?

In my imagination, the tiny mongrels sleep in handmade cribs wearing tiny diapers instead of being walked at night, which sparks another question: *Why aren't these dogs walking?* Isn't this what canines are meant to do? To walk, run and sniff where other dogs have been and then to lift their tiny legs to relieve themselves in the same place? They aren't frail like their owners. They appear in robust health.

"Well, we must be going," the woman says. "We'll be late for the dog groomers."

My eyes widen. I can't begin to imagine why these dogs need to be groomed. They are already more presentable than I am.

"Enjoy your walk," I say to the elder couple, since it seems Scarlett and Rhett are out of luck.

Before I leave, Scarlett winks like her southern vixen namesake and a bejeweled Rhett raises his head, his bow tie slightly askew, and a panting smile on his face. As the man lowers the curtain, Rhett's smile fades and his eyes plead for rescue. I offer an apologetic look.

Aren't we all captured by love in one way or another? At least he has a nice set of wheels.

The Secret Sense of Wildflower

(a short story based on the novel)

The church was sweltering. It was three o'clock on an August afternoon with not a hint of breeze. Preacher clutched a worn, black Bible and bellowed out the 23rd psalm like we were all half-deaf. Sweat formed in large half-moon circles under his arms. Droplets danced on his wide forehead as if the fires of hell nipped at his dusty black shoes. He was bald except for a thin, sagging crescent of dull brown hair that reached from one ear to the other, a temporary dam for the sweat, before it streamed down his neck.

Poised to catch all the best gossip, I sat between Mama and my older sister, Meg. My other two sisters and our Aunt Sadie filled out the pew where our family always sat. It was our second funeral that year, and I stared at the wooden box containing Ruby Monroe. It smelled of new lumber and hardly seemed big enough for a girl my age. I worried that her legs were cramped up under her and that she didn't have on shoes. The Monroe family was one of the poorest in Katy's Ridge.

Nobody was sure what killed Ruby, though rumors were as thick as molasses. If a person could die of misery, that would be my guess. But if anybody knew what really happened it would be my sister, Meg.

As if reading my thoughts, Meg leaned forward and whispered to Mama, "Ruby hung herself."

Covering my mouth, I swallowed a gasp. I'd heard of criminals getting hung, but I'd never known anybody to do it to themselves. Especially somebody I'd just seen at Abbott's store three days earlier. Ruby had stood in front of the counter barefooted, her feet muddy, counting out pennies to Mr. Abbott to buy a sack of flour. Her stomach stuck out, like poor people's do when they don't get enough to eat. I'd said hello and she gave me a quick nod before looking away.

"They found Ruby swinging in an oak tree," Meg whispered.

My eyes widened.

"That poor child," Mama whispered back.

I closed my eyes and pictured Ruby with her sad eyes and muddy feet, swinging by the neck from a tree she probably played in as a little girl. My stomach lurched and I had to remind myself to breathe.

"God rest her soul," Mama said.

"God rest her soul," Meg echoed.

"God rest her soul," I added to the chorus of whispers.

"But that's not the worst of it," Meg began again. She kept an eye on Preacher so she could stop if he noticed she wasn't listening.

"What could be worse?" Mama asked.

I wondered the same.

"She was . . . in a family way," Meg said in her softest voice.

Mama looked over my head at Meg. She could say more with her eyes than a whole dictionary full of words.

'In a family way' meant Ruby's stomach wasn't just big from being hungry. Tears filled my eyes for Ruby Monroe and for her baby who would never see the light of day. Then questions crowded my mind. Why would Ruby do such a thing? How could she possibly be so desperate and scared? And who was the father of her baby? I'd never seen any boys around her. I knew only one thing for sure. If this had happened to me, I wouldn't have to kill myself because Mama would do it for me.

Mr. Monroe, Ruby's father, lounged on the front row wearing a pair of torn overalls, his dirty hat staying on his head the whole time and no one willing to make him take it off. I'd never seen him in church, and he looked about as out of place as a mule in a kitchen. He took out his pocketknife, opened the blade swiftly with his thumb and scraped at the dirt caked on the bottom of his boots, letting the dirt fall onto the clean church floor.

Johnny, Ruby's older brother, slouched next to him, staring at the floor, his hair uncombed. His younger sister, Melody, leaned into Johnny's arm. Her nose was always running and she looked younger than her years. I'd never known this family to have a mother in it. I'd heard tell she ran off.

There were two things I was afraid of. One was dying young, as Ruby had just done, the other was Johnny Monroe. Whenever I saw Johnny a creepy feeling crawled the length of my spine. Daddy used to say that fear was a friend that taught us that life wasn't to be played with. Friends like that I could live without.

At sixteen, Johnny was a good six inches taller than me, even slouched. Shreds of chewing tobacco were caked around the edges of his teeth. But the scariest thing was the look he got in his eyes whenever he saw me coming down the road. He was like a wildcat. Mountain people knew that anytime you came across a wildcat you didn't look it in the eye or make any sudden moves. Every time I saw Johnny Monroe I slowed down and stared at the tops of my shoes.

Sweat stuck my legs to the wooden bench as I thought of poor Ruby Monroe inside that box. Preacher's voice echoed against the rafters as he told of God calling his children home when they least expected it. A trickle of sweat slid between my shoulder blades. If God decided to call me home anytime soon, I wasn't going to answer.

Preacher finished and wiped the perspiration from his face with a starched white handkerchief. In a flourish of wrong notes, Miss Mildred played *Amazing Grace* real slow on the old church organ. We all sang along, most of the congregation confident that Ruby Monroe was the wretch that needed saving and since she never came to church, she was out of luck.

After the music stopped, the four McClure brothers went up front and lifted Ruby's pine box. The youngest McClure boy grunted, as if the box weighed more than he expected. They balanced their load and we filed out of the church, following the box up the hill to the cemetery. In the distance a pile of fresh red dirt marked Ruby's final resting place, a stone's throw away from Daddy's willow tree.

Daddy had one of those markers in the graveyard where if you subtracted the years, you figured he was thirty-four when he died eleven months ago. Once a week I walked up the hill and lazed under the willow tree and told him about things going on in my life. He'd be sad to hear about Ruby.

I was the only girl I knew who hung out in graveyards. But if you didn't mind being around dead people, it had a beautiful view overlooking the river. Thick, old maples and oaks graced the hillside and the nearby stream emptied into the river at the bottom of the hill. In the distance stood the small, white Baptist church practically everybody in Katy's Ridge attended. The large weeping willow grew in the center of the graveyard. Its leaves swept the ground when the wind blew like Mama swept the porch in the evenings. Last fall it had wept almond-shaped gold leaves on top of Daddy's grave, and I knew he must have been smiling because he always said he'd struck gold when I was born.

Daddy was the one who nicknamed me "Wildflower." He said it fit me perfect since I'd sprung up here in the mountains like a wild trillium. Trilliums would take your breath away if you saw a patch of them. Daddy had a way with words, like a poet, and not just with me. He had made Mama smile all the time and could make her laugh so hard tears would stream out of her eyes. All us kids would stand around with our jaws dropped because to see Mama laugh was as rare as snow in August.

Sometimes I wondered if Mama ever got mad at him for going away. I know I did. After the sadness gnawed me numb, I got pissed as a rattlesnake that he hadn't been more careful at the sawmill. All it had taken was that one mistake to leave us all alone to fend for ourselves.

The melody of *Amazing Grace* played in my head as we followed Ruby Monroe's pine box up the hill. Aunt Sadie squeezed my hand like she remembered the last time we had climbed this hill together. Aunt Sadie was Daddy's sister. She had a long braid of silver hair that she sat on if she wasn't careful. I had a secret sense she knew exactly what I was feeling. The secret sense, according to Aunt Sadie, was a nudge from somewhere deep inside that told you things you wouldn't ordinarily know. She said it was how one heart talked to another. You could be as stupid as all get out, but your secret sense was always wise.

Aunt Sadie was full of ideas that most people didn't cater to. Not to mention she had never married, which made some people nervous, and she wore a man's hat nearly everywhere she went. She kept to herself most of the time and collected herbs and roots from all over the mountains to make her remedies. People came from all over to have her doctor them with red clover blossoms and honey to cure their whooping cough or to get catnip mint to soothe their colicky babies. She also made the best blackberry wine in three counties.

A fine, misty rain started to fall. The McClure brothers lowered Ruby's box into the hole with two ropes. Preacher got out his Bible again.

"Ashes to ashes, dust to dust," he said, tossing a clump of red dirt into the hole.

The dirt hit Ruby's coffin with a dull thud and Mama turned her head away and glanced off into the distance at Daddy's grave. As far as I knew, she hadn't visited his grave once since he died. I wanted to take her by the hand and lead her there and show her how beautiful it was. But when her eyes got ominous and gray, it was best to leave her alone. Meanwhile, the rain grew harder and thunder rumbled in the distance, as we said our final goodbyes to Ruby Monroe.

Later that day I went to change out of my Sunday clothes while Mama made supper. When I returned to the kitchen, a large bowl of pinto beans sat on the table next to an iron skillet of cornbread. The skillet rested on folded dishrags so it wouldn't burn the wood. Next to the cornbread was a big plate of sliced tomatoes that Mama grew out in the side yard. After we said grace, I speared three slices with my fork and put them on my plate. We ate like this a lot since Daddy died.

Mama could make even a bowl of pinto beans taste like a feast. Mixed in with the beans were pieces of ham, sweet onion and turnip greens.

Jo and Amy, my two older sisters were married and lived right down the road from our house. Meg, my closest sister in age, graduated from high school but still lived at home and worked at the Woolworth's store in Rocky Bluff, thirty minutes away. I liked having Meg around. She smoothed things out between Mama and me. Since Daddy died, even on our best days, we were like vinegar and soda, always reacting. When Meg wasn't there, Mama and I did our level best to avoid each other.

Little Women was Mama's favorite book. A worn copy of it rested on her dresser next to the Bible. I was named after the lady who wrote it, Louisa May Alcott. Destiny must have rewarded Mama for her devotion because she gave Daddy four daughters, just like the March family. My older sisters, Amy, Jo, and Meg, were each named after somebody in the book. Another sister, Beth, died two days after she was born. That explained how I ended up with the name Louisa May. All the good names were already taken.

"Tell me the latest gossip from the Woolworth's," Mama said to Meg, resting her chin in her hand. Hearing about other people's troubles seemed to distract her from her own. While Mama soaked in the idle chatter, I sneaked a third piece of cornbread, thankfully missing her speech on gluttony. When she got riled up, Mama could sound just like Preacher.

"Don't you have something to do?" Mama said to me. She didn't wait for an answer.

I cleared the table and took the dishes to the sink to wash, a job I'd inherited after Amy left home. It was a chore I didn't mind since I could let my mind wander while I stood at the kitchen sink. Pondering came natural to me. I could sit and be entertained by my thoughts for enormous amounts of time. Mama called this just being lazy.

After I scraped the leftovers into a rusty pie tin, I took it out back to feed the stray cats that lived under our house. Daddy started this tradition, but Mama didn't like it.

"Your daddy was just too soft hearted with those cats," she said. "If he'd had his way about it, he would have attracted every stray cat in the state of Tennessee."

"Yes, Mama." She said the same thing every night.

"Well, you're lucky I don't drown them all."

This threat was new and she looked at me as if wanting to register the level of my shock. But I felt too tired to fight, and didn't let my face tell her anything. Not all the cats stayed after Daddy died. But the ones that did ran from Mama every time they saw her. Even cats could sense when they weren't wanted.

A new kitten showed up the day Ruby died. Small and orange, he didn't mind being touched. As I sat on the steps, he finished the little bits of food the other cats let him have and then weaved between my ankles.

"If you see Mama coming with a bucket, you run, okay?" I rubbed his whiskers and he soaked up my attention with a raspy purr.

Even though I was full of Mama's cornbread and beans, I felt empty when I thought about Daddy being in the graveyard instead of here on the back porch. Evenings were the worst because we used to sit together and he'd read stories to me or talk about how our people came over from other countries. Leaning against a post, I closed my eyes to remember the sound of his voice. I worried sometimes that I'd forget it and that my memories would go mute.

I left the back porch, passed Mama and Meg still in the kitchen and sat in the rocker in the living room near the wood stove Daddy bought from the Sears & Roebuck catalog when I was seven. Daddy's banjo—missing one string he didn't have time to replace—leaned against the wall nearby, right where he left it. Daddy used to sing country songs that told stories about people. His voice had been deep and rich and wrapped around me like one of Mama's softest quilts.

Quiet as a ghost, so Mama wouldn't get mad, I picked up Daddy's old banjo and returned to the rocker where he always sat to play. I pretended to pick at the strings and threw back my head like he used to. I hummed the words of *Down in the Valley, Valley so low*. At that moment the ache I felt in my stomach moved up to the center of my chest and my breathing caught in my throat. I didn't understand why anybody had to die, especially when they were young.

I sat there until the sun and shadows on the wall faded to darkness. When I got up from the rocking chair, I was careful not to let the chair's feet crackle on the wooden floor and put Daddy's banjo back in its spot where the dust kept the shape of it, so Mama wouldn't know I'd touched it.

"What are you doing here in the dark?" Mama asked.

Most of the things Mama said to me were either orders or questions, neither of which ever required an answer. I shrugged and shuffled to the bedroom I shared with Meg who was already snoring like a sailor.

After I put on my nightgown, I couldn't quit thinking about Ruby and Daddy. I walked down the hall toward Mama's room and found her sitting on the edge of the bed brushing her hair. Her hair reached midway down her back and was the color of spun honey. It was much prettier down instead of up in the tight bun she wore during the day.

"Can I sleep with you?" I asked. She looked at me kind of surprised, like the day I told her I had changed my name to Wildflower.

For a second her face softened and I imagined her pulling back the covers on Daddy's side of the bed while I jumped in. But then she said, "Don't be silly, Louisa May. You're practically grown up."

Her words stung like the bee I'd stepped on once, while barefooted in a patch of clover. I wanted to kick myself for even asking. Mama had changed since Daddy died, and I kept waiting on her to change back.

I returned to the bed I shared with Meg and climbed under the sheets. Out of pure meanness, I poked her in the ribs with my elbow until she slapped at me and told me to quit. Lying there in the dark, I counted backwards from a hundred by threes and tried not to think about Ruby Monroe in that cramped pine box under the ground. Or the fact that Daddy would never be coming home. Or my deepest, darkest, secret wish, wrapped tight in the covers of shame: that Mama had died instead of Daddy.

Thank you for reading!

Dear Reader,

I hope you enjoyed *Grace, Grits and Ghosts: Southern Short Stories*. I want you to know that I have loved writing these short stories over the last decade, and I have actually missed spending time with these southern characters now that they have journeyed out into the world.

As an author, I rely on your feedback to complete the circle as the story travels from writer to reader and then back again. To be honest, you're the reason I write. So feel free tell me what you liked, what you loved, even what you wish I'd done differently. You can also let me know if you want more stories like these. I'd love to hear from you!

You can write me at susan@susangabriel.com or visit my website at www.susangabriel.com.

Finally, I need to ask a favor.

If you're so inclined, please consider writing and posting a review of *Grace, Grits and Ghosts*. Whether you loved it or not, I'd appreciate your feedback. Reviews can be tough to come by these days, and you, the reader, have the power to champion a book or ignore it.

Whether you bought this book online or at your local bookstore you can review it at their website or Goodreads.

In your review, if you want, you can tell potential readers what you liked most about the book, what interested or surprised you, or whatever you feel like writing. It doesn't have to be long.

Thanks so much for reading *Grace, Grits and Ghosts* and for spending time with me.

With gratitude,
Susan Gabriel

P.S. Do you want to get notified when I publish new books? I would be happy to email you as soon as new books are available (two to three times a year at most). Please sign up here today: https://www.susangabriel.com/new-books/

Interview with Susan Gabriel

(This interview was first posted at Quixotic Magpie in 2012)

Is anything in your books based on real life experiences or purely all imagination?

I had a huge debate over this with a screenwriter once. She swore that none of her work was autobiographical, but my argument was that our work can't help but be autobiographical, simply in terms of what we notice as writers. I notice sounds and smells and see things in a way that is totally unique to me. My imagination is the instrument I use to tell a story, so it can't help but be a reflection of me in some way. Length of paragraphs, turn of phrase, word choice, my choice of metaphors are all, in a way, my tiny fingerprint. That said, none of the fiction I write is my personal story.

Is there any particular author or book that influenced you in any way either growing up or as an adult?

The Grapes of Wrath by John Steinbeck blew me away the first time I read it. I wanted to be able to write like that someday. And, of course, I loved *To Kill a Mockingbird*. As someone born and raised in the South, this book really spoke to me. A

Kirkus reviewer compared the main character in *The Secret Sense of Wildflower* to an adolescent Scout Finch. This was a great compliment to me.

Do you work with an outline, or just write?

I am what is called an intuitive writer. *The Secret Sense of Wildflower* started with a voice, eleven years ago, at four in the morning. A voice that woke me up from a deep sleep. It was the voice of a girl who began to tell me her story:

"There are two things I'm afraid of," she said. "One is dying young. The other is Johnny Monroe."

A day or two before, I had visited the small cemetery located in the southern Appalachian Mountains where many of my family are buried. I spent an afternoon walking among the final resting places of my grandparents, aunts, uncles and cousins, as well as ancestors I had never known. Had I accidentally brought one of them home with me, who needed her story told?

Rest assured, mental illness does not run in my family. But for a fiction writer, to get the voice of a character so clearly is really good news. I, however, wanted to go back to sleep. Who wouldn't, at 4 o'clock in the morning? For a time, I debated whether or not to get up. I ultimately decided that the voice might find someone else to write her story if I didn't claim it.

Needless to say, I turned on the light, picked up a pen and a pad of paper and began to write the story of Louisa May

"Wildflower" McAllister. It took months of listening to her and seeing the scenes of her life play out in my imagination. Then it took years of revising and revisiting the story to polish it and get it ready to share with readers.

I have seen photos of famous authors' offices where they write, and stood in Hemingway's office. What is the environment like where you write?

I live in the mountains of North Carolina, so everywhere I look are oak trees, wild dogwoods, birds and an occasional deer. In the winter, I can see seven mountain ridges. In the summer, it's just a blur of green. My office has two giant windows and just off my office is a screened-in porch, so when it's warm enough I have the sliding glass doors open to the outside. I am very lucky that I live in such a beautiful place. I live a humble life, but the setting is amazing and inspiring, which really helps since I spend a lot of time at home writing. That said, I also know that I can write anywhere. It isn't about setting. It's about sitting still long enough to get the work done.

Laptop or desktop or iPad?

Laptop for writing something new. Desktop for putting in edits. Various comfortable chairs around the house depending on the season, both inside and outside. I follow the sun in winter and seek out shade in summer. Also, I have a favorite coffee shop I escape to whenever I want to get out of the house.

What has been the best compliment you've received as a writer?

I've had readers say they've lost sleep because they can't put my books down. That's always a good sign and a huge compliment to a writer. It means the story has kept them engaged.

Also, they tell me that they were sorry when the story was over. They wanted it to go on and on.

I suppose the biggest compliment I get from readers is that they read my books! It helps that I'm pretty accessible through my website and blog so people find it easy to email me and tell me how moved they were by one of my books. Some will tell me that one of the characters gave them courage or hope in their own lives. That means a lot.

If readers take the time to email me, it is usually because they really liked the book and they'll tell me why. I cherish these emails.

On a professional level, to review a starred review from Kirkus Reviews was a big deal for me. I've been writing in utter obscurity for so many years and been rejected a zillion times, so to have such a respected reviewer call *The Secret Sense of Wildflower* "a book of remarkable merit" and for it to be chosen as a Best Book of 2012 will keep me going for years. But truly, it's the readers' comments that mean even more to me.

What project are you working on now?

I am revising a novel called *Circle of the Ancestors* that I wrote a few years ago. It will be a joy to revisit the characters. I've missed them. It's set here in the mountains of North Carolina on the Cherokee Indian Reservation. It has a wise woman in it and her grandson who finds a priceless star ruby in the roots of a tree and must decide what to do with this treasure. This is the first book I wrote where I realized how important ancestors were to me. They have ended up being a theme in later books, too. *[Circle of the Ancestors was published in 2014.]*

What do you do when you are not writing?

I take walks by a river that flows through Pisgah National Forest. I hang out in coffee shops with friends and talk about books and writing and whatever our current passions are. I also spend a lot of time reading...no surprise...and watch a lot of films. I love figuring out what makes a story work and what causes one to miss the mark. I enjoy listening to professional storytellers when I have an opportunity, as well. I love good stories in all forms.

Finally, for fun, chocolate or vanilla?

Definitely chocolate, preferably with almonds. Yum.

Tea or coffee?

Organic Assam tea, loose leaf. A part of my every day writing ritual: make myself a pot of tea.

*   *   *

Other Books by Susan Gabriel

"A quietly powerful story, at times harrowing, but ultimately a joy to read." - Kirkus Reviews, starred review (for books of remarkable merit)

Named to Kirkus Reviews' Best Books of 2012.

Set in 1940s Appalachia, *The Secret Sense of Wildflower* tells the story of Louisa May "Wildflower" McAllister whose life has been shaped around the recent death of her beloved father in a sawmill accident. While her mother hardens in her grief, Wildflower and her three sisters must cope with their loss themselves, as well as with the demands of daily survival. Despite these hardships, Wildflower has a resilience that is forged with humor, a love of the land, and an endless supply of questions to God. When Johnny Monroe, the town's teenage ne'er-do-well, sets his sights on Wildflower, she must draw on the strength of her relations, both living and dead, to deal with his threat.

With prose as lush and colorful as the American South, *The Secret Sense of Wildflower* is a powerful and poignant southern novel, brimming with energy and angst, humor and hope.

Praise for *The Secret Sense of Wildflower*

"Louisa May immerses us in her world with astute observations and wonderfully turned phrases, with nary a cliché to be found. She could be an adolescent Scout Finch, had Scout's father died unexpectedly and her life taken a bad turn...By necessity, Louisa May grows up quickly, but by her secret sense, she also understands forgiveness. A quietly powerful story, at times harrowing but ultimately a joy to read." – Kirkus Reviews

"A soulful narrative to keep the reader emotionally charged and invested. *The Secret Sense of Wildflower* is eloquent and moving tale chock-filled with themes of inner strength, family and love." – Maya Fleischmann, indiereader.com

"I've never read a story as dramatically understated that sings so powerfully and honestly about the sense of life that stands in tribute to bravery as Susan Gabriel's, *The Secret Sense of Wildflower*...When fiction sings, we must applaud." – T. T. Thomas, author of *A Delicate Refusal*

"The story is powerful, very powerful. Excellent visuals, good drama. I raced to get to the conclusion...but didn't really want to read the last few pages because then it would be over! I look forward to Gabriel's next offering." – Nancy Purcell, Author

"Just finished this with tears streaming down my face. Beautifully written with memorable characters who show resilience in the face of tragedy. I couldn't put this down and will seek Susan Gabriel's other works. This is truly one of the best books I've read in a very long time." – A.C.

"An interesting story enhanced by great writing, this book was a page turner. It captures life in the Tennessee mountains truthfully but not harshly. I would recommend this book to anyone who enjoys historical fiction." – E. Jones

"I don't even know how to tell you what I love about this book --- the incredible narrator? The heartbreaking and inspiring storyline? The messages about hope, wisdom, family and strength? All of those!! Everything about it!" – K. Peck

"Lovely, soul stirring novel. I absolutely could not put it down! Beautifully descriptive, evocative story told in the voice of Wildflower, a young girl of the mountains, set in a wild yet beautiful 1940's mountain town, holds you captive from the start. I had to wait to write my review, as I was crying too hard to see!" – V.C.

"I write novels, too, but this writer is fantastic. The story is authentic and gripping. Her voice through the child, Wildflower, is captivating. This story would make a great movie. I love stories that portray life changing tragedy and pain coupled with power of the human spirit to survive and continue to love and forgive. Bravo! Susan. Please write more and more." – Judi D.

"This is a wonderful story that will make you laugh, cry, and cheer." –T.B. Markinson

"I was pretty blown away by how good this book is. I didn't read it with any expectations, hadn't heard anything about it really, so when I read it, I realized from page one that it is a well written, powerful book." – Quixotic Magpie

"If you liked Little Women or if you love historical fiction and coming-of-age novels, this is the book for you. Definitely add The Secret Sense of Wildflower to your TBR pile; you won't regret it." – PandaReads

"Bottom line: A great story about a strong character!" – Meg, A Bookish Affair

Temple Secrets

A novel

Fans of *The Help* and *Midnight in the Garden of Good and Evil* will delight in this comic novel of family secrets by acclaimed writer, Susan Gabriel.

Every family has secrets, but the elite Temple family of Savannah has more than most. To maintain their influence, they've also been documenting the indiscretions of other prestigious southern families, dating as far back as the Civil War. When someone begins leaking these tantalizing tidbits to the newspaper, the entire city of Savannah, Georgia is rocking with secrets.

The current keeper of the secrets and matriarch of the Temple clan is Iris, a woman of unpredictable gastrointestinal illnesses and an extra streak of meanness that even the ghosts in the Temple mansion avoid. When Iris unexpectedly dies, the consequences are far flung and significant, not only to her family—who get in line to inherit the historic family mansion—but to Savannah itself.

At the heart of the story is Old Sally, an expert in Gullah folk magic, who some suspect cast a voodoo curse on Iris. At 100 years of age, Old Sally keeps a wise eye over the whole boisterous business of secrets and the settling of Iris's estate.

In the Temple family, nothing is as it seems, and everyone has a secret.

Available in paperback, ebook and audiobook.

Praise for *Temple Secrets*

"Temple Secrets is a page-turner of a story that goes deeper than most on the subjects of equality, courage and dignity. There were five or six characters to love and a few to loathe. Gabriel draws Queenie, Violet, Spud and Rose precisely, with a narrative dexterity that is amazingly and perfectly sparse while achieving an impact of fullness and depth. Their interactions with the outside world and one another are priceless moments of hilarious asides, well-aimed snipes and a plethora of sarcasms.

"What happens when the inevitable inequities come about amongst the Haves, the Have Nots and the Damn-Right-I-Will-Have? When some people have far too much time, wealth and power and not enough humanness and courage? Oh, the answers Gabriel provides are as delicious as Violet's peach turnovers, and twice as addicting! I highly recommend this novel." – T.T. Thomas

"Susan Gabriel shines once again in this fascinating tale of a family's struggle to break free from their past. Filled with secrets, betrayals, and tragedy, the author weaves an intricate storyline that will keep you hooked." - R. Krug

"I loved this book! I literally couldn't put it down. The characters are fabulous and the story line has plenty of twists and turns making it a great read. I was born and raised in the south so I have an affinity for stories that are steeped in the southern culture. Temple Secrets nails it. All I needed was a glass of sweet tea to go with it." – Carol Clay

"The setting is rich and sensuous, and the secrets kept me reading with avid interest until most of them were revealed. I read the book in just a few days because I really didn't want to put it down. It is filled with characters who are funny, tragic, unpredictable and nuanced, and I must admit that I really came to know and love some of them by the end of the story." – Nancy Richards

"I was glued from the first moment that I began reading. The book accurately portrays many of the attitudes of the Old South including the intricate secrets and "skeletons in the closet" that people often wish to deny. Each character is fascinating and I loved watching each one evolve as the story unfolded. This was one of those books that I did not want to finish as it was so much fun to be involved in the action." – Lisa Patty

"I just finished reading Temple Secrets today and I truly hated for it to end! Susan Gabriel writes with such warmth and humor, and this book is certainly no exception. I loved getting to know the characters and the story was full of humor and suspense." – Carolyn Tenn

Fiction

The Secret Sense of Wildflower
(a Kirkus Reviews Best Book of 2012)

Lily's Song
(sequel to *The Secret Sense of Wildflower*)

Temple Secrets

Trueluck Summer

Seeking Sara Summers

Circle of the Ancestors

Quentin & the Cave Boy

Nonfiction

Fearless Writing for Women:
Extreme Encouragement & Writing Inspiration

Available at all booksellers
in print, ebook and audio formats.

About the Author

Susan Gabriel is an acclaimed writer who lives in the mountains of North Carolina. Her novel, *The Secret Sense of Wildflower*, earned a starred review ("for books of remarkable merit") from Kirkus Reviews and was selected as one of their Best Books of 2012.

She is also the author of *Temple Secrets*, *Lily's Song* and other novels. Discover more about Susan at SusanGabriel.com.

CPSIA information can be obtained
at www.ICGtesting.com
Printed in the USA
BVOW08s0523070717
488545BV00002B/153/P